To Bethney.
For tasting all my demons,
and liking them.

Montag Press
ISBN: 978-1-940233-21-5
Jacket and book design © 2015 Rick Febré
Author photo © 2015 Beth Coleman

Montag Press Team:
Project Editor – Charlie Franco
Polish Editor – Mara Hodges
Managing Director – Charlie Franco

A Montag Press Book
www.montagpress.com
Montag Press
1066 47th Ave. Unit #9
Oakland CA 94601 USA

Montag Press, the burning book with the hatchet cover, the skewed word mark and the portrayal of the long-suffering fireman mascot are trademarks of Montag Press.
Printed & Digitally Originated in the United States of America
10 9 8 7 6 5 4 3 2 1

WOUND

A N D

SUTURE

SHORT STORIES BY W.A.COLEMAN

MONTAG

Several short stories have also appeared in the following publications

Salting Slugs (Evergreen Review, Issue 124, Sept 2010 and Twisted Tongue, Issue 14)

Two Fifty (Evergreen Review, Issue 119, Aug 2009)

A Love Trumping Lust (The Fringe Magazine, Dec 3, 2010)

Killers (House of Horror, July 2010, Issue 13)

Primal (Full of Crow, Jan. 2011)

Better This Way (The Houston Literary Review, March 2011)

Deicide 6 (Crack the Spine, May 2012)

Kiss' Bliss (Echo Ink Review, Vol. 4.1, Dec 2012)

A Judgment's Sonnet (3:AM Magazine, July 24, 2012)

God's Song (The Used Furniture Review, upcoming)

The Giver (Fiction 365, May 22, 2013)

One More Round (The Rusty Nail, Jan 2013)

Last Summer Snow (Foundling Review, Jan. 2011, Issue 1)

WOUND

A N D

SUTURE

SHORT STORIES BY W.A. COLEMAN

WOUND

Salting Slugs

One of my favorite things to do is to salt slugs. I stand out on my front porch, overlooking my tomato garden, where they gather year-round, and with my big cup of coffee and my egg-shaped shaker, I rain salt down on those nasty little creatures. Watching them convulse until they spasm so hard they flip up off the ground brings a smile to my face every morning.

I've always been a little different and I don't mean in a unique snowflake kind of way. You know the people who make the world a better place? I'm the opposite of that. Even my very conception was proof of that; not only was I never destined to bring any joy into this world but I wasn't really invited in the first place.

My mother recalls having a drink in a shady night club with a tall, handsome man with a dragon tattoo on his right forearm. The next thing she remembers is waking up at the Motel 6 down the dusty strip with a bruised crotch and a groggy head. Police said it was probably Gamma Hydroxybutyric Acid, Ketamine or Rohypnol, commonly known on the street as Roofie, Cherry Meth or Easy Lay, depending on what neighborhood you're in when you buy it. The only thing Dad left her was about ten black pubic hairs and yours truly.

She should have terminated the pregnancy immediately. I know she wanted to and I don't blame her for that. Hell, if it was me, I'd have been bending hangers on the way to the clinic just in case I got stuck in traffic. But the fear of eternal damnation was a powerful one, especially around here. So she did what everyone told her she should do: she went on with the pregnancy and according to them, she was a strong, brave woman because of it. She was a woman following God's will. I guess if God can make the Earth in seven days, He can probably possess a crazed date rapist to impregnate my mom. But He really should have thought it through a bit more or, at least, had me take after *her*.

The older I got the more of my father started to surface. I was the type of girl who, by the time I was fourteen, had my leg propped up on the toilet bowl and was masturbating furiously to some ragged early eighties playgirl magazine splayed out on the wet bathroom floor. I'd steal and smuggle any type of smut, from Honcho to Cheri from my friend's parent's house and lust over them like a teenage boy. By fifteen, I had given more blowjobs than a catholic schoolgirl and was already the proud owner of a high-powered vibrator.

I'd go to Senior parties and hang around all the big, drunk football players just waiting for one of them to take advantage of me. But I learned my lesson early on; when you look at a high school kid dead in the eye and say, "Fuck me", they'll usually lose their nerve and turn into a shaking little virgin with a semi chub. What a letdown. That's when I figured out that if you act more scared, timid and lady-like, you get fucked more. Funny how that is.

Just to be clear here, I wasn't acting like some slut just to get the guys to like me. This was no cry for help. I just love sex. It's that simple. There's a difference between fucking to get a guy to like you and then fucking because your pussy's been wet for so long that you fear dehydration will set in if you don't plug the hole. If there was one thing that I could wish for, I just wish I attracted more of the shallow, horny types. These days, it seems like most men are mentally prepared to go two or three dates before trying to get in your pants, so if I want to get pounded, I have to embrace being a slut in order to re-program guys into accepting the fact that, yes, this is our first date and yes, I am sucking on your balls.

The other day this guy took me out to dinner and a movie. Boring, but he was pretty hot, having the whole Mark Walberg thing going on. And he was a little taller. I hate short men. His big, plump veins pushed up against his skin and wrapped around his muscular, meaty forearms like grayish-blue ropes. He was nice, sweet and very gentlemanly, but I knew from the way he was looking at me that all he really wanted was to fuck my brains out and that was exactly what I wanted him to do. I just wish he didn't feel the need to put on that "good boy" act. God knows what uppity bitch he was dating before. Too many women believe that their pussies are so special that they've created an elaborate screening process just to let a guy get a sneak peek. It's almost like they are trying so hard to pretend that they don't even like cock. But that's fine with me. It leaves more for me, and where I'm from I can't be too picky, since the pickings get awfully slim. I'm just too horny to put my pussy on a pedestal. Hell, just watching his big, thick fingers being lubricated from the handfuls of buttery popcorn made me wish he was more of a presumptuous asshole. It made me regret not being back in high school when the boys were so unabashedly horny and impatient they were trying to get their buttery fingers inside you before the previews were over.

I know they say chivalry is already dead but would someone please, go outside, dig it up and shoot it again for me and quickly, because I'm losing fluids.

As my sexual habits have developed over the years, I've realized that I am definitely a daddy's girl. I'm just lucky guys are willing to give it up easy enough that I don't have to drug them.

Besides, I don't know what a slip of Mexican Valium would do to a perfectly stiff cock. I don't want to be on top of an unconscious guy trying to stuff a marshmallow in a piggy bank, if you get my drift.

Ten years ago I got a call from a detective claiming that a man in Albuquerque, who they'd arrested, admitted to the drugging and rape of my mother in Texas. He said they could confirm this if I'd be willing to do a DNA test. They were right. He was my biological father. I asked for a picture of him. He was older than I had imagined, but he had my same colorings, and we shared the same large black eyes.

I went to his trial and sat in the crowd. I don't really know why. I guess I just wanted to see him in person. I wanted to hear him talk, see him walk, and learn about him. Turns out, he wasn't just my mother's rapist. He was a mass murderer with killings of both men and women stretching all the way from Illinois down to Oklahoma. If I said his name, you'd know of him.

During the trial, I watched him like I watch porn. I didn't blink. I memorized everything I could during the week-long trial from how he scratched his nose to how uncomfortable he felt in that rented three-piece suit. I listened to the families of the victims as they verbally bludgeoned him while holding up pictures of their lost loved ones. I couldn't help but roll my eyes at each family's impassioned pleas for vengeance because they were wasting their time. The familiar, hollow look in his dark eyes, paired with that chilling and relaxed swagger, even as the judge sentenced my father to death, showed a man who was not at all remorseful. I hoped the victims' emotional venting helped them personally because all he did was casually smirk when they condemned him to Hell. Even Hell couldn't make him care.

Out of all my father's characteristics, it was that complete indifference that rang the most familiar to me. When I was a little girl, the neighbor's pit bull killed my new kitten right in front of my eyes. It completely mutilated the thing. Instead of crying for my dead kitten, I calmly walked in the garage, grabbed a bottle of lighter fluid, and got the bar matches from the mantel. I shook the neighbor's flimsy, chain link fence until the stupid dog ran over barking and snapping like he always did. While standing on my tiptoes, I just barely reached over the fence and drenched the dog with so much lighter fluid that he thought it was a game. He was jumping up, trying to bite the clear stream of lighter fluid, giving me ample opportunity to douse him from head to tail. The first match didn't work. I was surprised. But I threw a second one that crackled to light perfectly and, in an instant, I had a walking, crying, four-legged bonfire. I didn't know dogs could scream until that day. He ran around the yard for several seconds until he finally slowed down and fell over. I sat there with a grin on my face and watched the canine burn. The thing that really bothered me about the whole ordeal was the nasty smell of burnt hair. Other than that, the only thing I felt was complete and total satisfaction. I believed that I had done my kitten justice. But, still, I remember clearly that I didn't miss or even mourn for my furry little pussy cat, even at that young age. In fact, after I got up to return the lighter fluid and matches to their rightful place, I clearly remember being happy that I wouldn't have to clean the kitty litter anymore.

After that day, with the neighbor threatening to burn our house down, my step-dad was pretty convinced that I was the Antichrist with a vagina and my mom didn't know whether to shit or go blind. Again, I can't blame them. That's a lot of pre-meditation for an eight-year-old.

"Now what did you do this summer, young lady?"
Answering that question honestly with regards to my neigh-

bor's dog to my third grade teacher wasn't a smart move either. Consequently, I believe that's why I never got the *student of the month* gold star stickers on the class board.

What makes matters worse is that, as I got older, not only did I become more comfortable with violence, but when puberty hit, I discovered a real organic attraction to it. I mean violence itself made me so *freakin'* hot.

When I was sixteen, I watched a stocky, quiet, dark-eyed kid named Eli beat the shit out of my boyfriend in the bowling alley parking lot. My big, handsome captain of the football team date looked like a soggy piece of bread out there fighting that crazy animal. That night, after leaving my boyfriend in the emergency room, I vividly remember being so turned on by the fight that I couldn't think straight. I wanted to hate Eli for what he had done, but the truth was that I couldn't shake those images of his stout muscular body pinning my boyfriend's arms down with his knees and pounding his face in, staining his knuckles red.

As I walked to my car, a box of musty light in the corner dark ER parking lot caught my eye. I noticed an old frayed Yellow Pages through the dirty window of a lit phone booth. I don't even remember looking up his name and address up or writing it down. All I remember is jetting past the exit to my house with his address so burned into my memory I can still recall it to this day.

When I knocked on his shady apartment door, the hollow sound echoed across the deathly silent complex. I had to adjust my panties because they were sticking to my crotch like a wet t-shirt on fake tits. He opened the door suddenly: shirtless, standing there thick and muscular, holding a bag of frozen corn on his swollen knuckles. He looked at me hard, then gave me a suspicious grin as he scooted to the side to let me in. I noticed that some of my boyfriend's blood was still on his chest and I almost came right there. Shivers went down my spine when I heard him shut and lock the door, not from fear but from sexual excitement: the only feeling I really ever have.

I was well aware of his reputation. I knew he was older, way too old for me. I also knew from the stories that I had heard that he was dangerous and very sexually aggressive to women, but that was exactly what I was craving. We never said a word to each other. He never asked what I wanted or why I was there. He just grabbed my ninety-eight pound body and threw me on this ancient, swollen and stained mattress. He didn't just take my sleazy dress off, he ripped it off and he didn't start slow either; he just spread my legs and ate my pussy like it was his first meal in days. He fucked like he fought: skillfully, fast, and mercilessly. He only briefly flinched at my willingness to hand my body over on a silver platter. Even though he fucked me so hard that I could barely walk for days, I never saw him again. I think I scared him away. It's just as well. It's not like I wanted a relationship with him or anything. Sadly, though, he wouldn't be the last man I'd run off.

In college, I got pregnant by my professor and when he nervously suggested an abortion my response was, "Sure". I was young and he was married. I may have been a slut but I had no desire to be some home-wrecking bitch. I didn't want him to marry me; I didn't want his kid or his money. I wanted his big cock and an A in Calculus. I got both. But getting pregnant, to me, wasn't fate; it was a broken condom and a minor nuisance.

The nearest clinic was over 100 miles away. With his envelope of cash in hand, I was surprised at how friendly and kind everyone was. It was such a soothing and non-judgmental environment that I jokingly asked if there was a discount for the second one. They didn't laugh, but I could tell they wanted to. Afterwards, I must admit, I did have a really awful night. Not because of the abortion but because I decided to stop at a ghetto

Chinese restaurant on the way home. I mean, *Jesus fucking Christ*, if the procedure didn't kill the baby, the violent diarrhea from the pan-fried noodle chow mein would have. Other than that, I slept sounder that night than a dead baby. And for all you pro-lifers out there, trust me, a child with my genetics wouldn't have helped your cause. If she was anything like me, she'd end up getting so many abortions that, by the time she was twenty, the walls of her uterus would have seen more death than a Nazi gas chamber.

After handing me the envelope of cash, my big-dicked Calculus professor never talked to me again. In class, he pretended he didn't even know me but I expected that. I think when you tell a guy you don't want his offspring, it creates some kind of carnal hatred. I never told a soul about our fling and his marriage went on. Maybe he was a little surprised by my coldness in terminating his child, but that's just me. I never got depressed; I never shed a tear over it, because I never cry over anything. Ever. Not even when my parents died.

I was barely eighteen when my parents kicked me out of the house and it wasn't a lesson of tough love. It was them, especially my mother, giving up on me. It was her washing her hands of her spawn of an unnatural daughter; her own walking, talking by-product of rape and violence. With me gone, they could focus on my sister: the token of light in their litter of darkness. My sister was a sweet, kind and loving kid. She was a caring person, conceived inside the sanctity of a Christian marriage between two consenting adults, the perfect recipe for a perfect daughter. My mother now had a real child of her own, one she could look at in the eyes and would not have to be reminded of the psycho who had defiled her so many years ago. It goes to show that even God can be an asshole sometimes. He just *had* to give *me* all of my dad's colorings and features, and he *had* to give my sister all of my mother's looks, just to drive his devilishness home a bit more.

I didn't blame my parents for what they did to me. They were the good old-fashioned, God-fearing type who were deathly afraid that my natural-born evil would somehow drag them down into their own personal hell on earth. So I guess, that being said, they just couldn't love me. It wasn't their fault. You can't love me and believe in Hell because if you do, you're going there. On the other hand, she had also conveniently forgotten the fact that half of me was her, but I guess even her own flesh and blood wasn't enough for her to love me.

On the bright side though, it also meant that no one expected me to cry at their funeral. Their plane had turned into a comet from the sky and crashed down to earth at like a million miles an hour. There were no whole bodies, just pieces everywhere. The caskets they buried were empty except for some keepsakes that their other daughter chose. To me it was like they went on vacation and they never came back. The whole funeral reminded me of a big budget, Sci-Fi summer block buster movie where the characters and robots look real and sound real, but your mind just doesn't care to get involved in the story.

I do wish I would have been able to talk to my biological father before he died. While on death row, he had written asking for a picture of me. This I gave him. I heard that he held onto my picture when they finally injected him to death. What was I supposed to make out of that? Did this cold-blooded, mass-murdering rapist actually love me? Could he love me, even if he had never met me, just from seeing me sit across from him in the courthouse, our identical eyes locked onto each others'? Did knowing that he had a daughter give him a comforting sense of immortality, like a part of him would live on? I wasn't with my mother when she died, but I can assure you she wasn't thinking of me in her last few seconds. So maybe, Dad deserves a little more respect than caskets filled with sentimental tchotchkes.

I am God's will after all. Like my father, I am the result of life's twisted balancing act and nothing more. I suppose that makes sense somehow. It seems logical that every time a loving, caring person is born into this world, there has to be someone down the hall who's giving birth to a living wrecking ball of society, someone whose destiny is destruction. I guess I am one of the ones who make good people look so good. White always shows up better on a black background.

But I didn't choose to be born. Sometimes I feel like a solitary, emotionless robot thrown into the middle of a bunch of emotionally normal people. Even so, I don't hate what I am. I don't know why I'm different, and while I don't lose too much sleep over it, I do have questions. I've often wondered why the sight of blood makes me hot. Or why, when I see a newborn baby, I feel absolutely nothing. Or why emotions like pity or remorse remain such a mystery to me. Also with regard to crying, I have so many questions. What does crying feel like? Is it an overwhelming feeling of emotion that is uncontrollable and inevitable, or can people stop it if they wanted to? Does it feel good? Does it feel like a release? Is it painful? I meant it when I said I've never cried, ever. Even as a baby, my mother used to say I would just look at her with an empty gaze or shriek until I gave my parents nightmares. People would ask her if I was sick or something. Even when the doctor smacked my ass at birth, all I did was cough.

If you think you have any answers to these questions, then I'm all ears. I'm also open to intelligent speculation. You won't hurt my feelings. I haven't any feelings to hurt. Just don't bother calling me soulless, evil, or a whore. It's not that it would be an incorrect definition of who I am - in fact it is a correct one, but I already know that and I'm a little too comfortable with it, so trying to make me feel guilty would be like trying to keep the funk off of a stripper pole – an impossible task. And for those of you that suggest therapy, I've already gone down that road. Unfortunately, the therapist was more interested in coming on my chest than in dealing with my mental issues. Not that I was complaining; it's just that I didn't need to pay two-fifty an hour for some PhD cock when I can get it a lot cheaper and a lot better by dressing like a slut at the local Gold's gym.

But you won't have any answers. No one ever does. The truth is that no one can help me. Sometimes we are just born the way we are and nothing can change that. It doesn't matter anyway. It's not like I'm a danger to society. I have no plans on going "Ted Bundy" on anyone despite my father's actions. I have never had that desire to hurt or kill any human being any more than you probably have casually fantasized about it. Maybe that was courtesy of my mother's normal genes keeping me from crossing that line of psychosis. But even if someday, homicidal fantasies slowly start to creep into my mind, they'd have to be pretty damn strong because I have absolutely no interest in living out the rest of my insignificant life in an eight-by-eight cell with no toilet privacy and biweekly anal rapings by some crusty old guard named Frank who hasn't washed his cock since the Reagan administration. No thanks. My toilet privacy is just way too sacred to me, and I like my cocks well-groomed, with just a hint of Lever 2000.

Right now, I guess I'm content with being only half evil and a full slut. The other day I experienced a fabulous orgasm during one of the new Disney movies, and I've taken up bunny killing with my new Sheridan pellet rifle. The little fuckers do a number on the neighbor's garden, so I have a socially acceptable excuse to murder them.

To be honest, for being a soulless bitch, things are going

pretty great. As long as I can keep up the bubbly and compassionate alter ego that you normal people seem so charmed by, I completely fly under your radar. You'll never think for a second that I'm the whore next door who let your "brilliant", college-bound, eighteen-year-old boy fuck me up the ass on your favorite bedspread. You'll look at my cute, harmless appearance and never suspect that I'm the reason why your stupid, yippy Chihuahua, the one who used to shit in people's backyards and mess up my rose bed, mysteriously never came home. Don't worry; I'm sure he found a new, loving family. Denial can help you sleep at night. Just don't dig too deep in my tomato garden.

But, you know, I've played the part of being normal for so long it just might be rubbing off on me. This morning during my usual garden routine, this major feeling of frustration and disappointment caused my bottom lip to quiver a bit just for an instant. I didn't cry but from what I've seen, this is a big precursor. Unfortunately, it was because I had run out of salt.

Two-Fifty

She forcefully inhales the man's hot, ashtray-flavored breath: the only thing strong enough to cover up his body odor. The music from the house party downstairs blares loudly causing the cheap flower pictures in the bedroom to vibrate on the wall. Beads of sweat drip off the man's balding forehead and rain down on her chest as he un-rhythmically fucks her on the old waterbed. The wooden frame of the aqua-filled mattress creaks with his every thrust, keeping her mind miles away from satisfaction. *"Who the hell still sleeps on a waterbed?"* she thinks to herself as she bites her bottom lip and scrunches her face in discomfort. A sense of relief comes across her as she feels his back muscles tense and his body becomes rigid. He picks up the pace, continuing to exhale his vile air up her nostrils while grabbing her hair aggressively and finishing off with some dominatrix-style bed talk, "That's it bitch, … you like that? … huh? … you like that, you fuckin' little whore?"

"Yeah, … yeah baby," she moans, her amateur acting performance well suited for the local community theater.

"OHHH, … GOD!" he says, his voice sounding more like an angry dog growl than a man's. Finally he cums into the professionally applied, extra thick Trojan condom as he pulls hard on her hair, wrenching her head back, making her yelp in pain. He closes his eyes and snarls his lip, giving her an intimate view of his brown teeth. Then it's over faster than it started. The man rolls his sweaty body off hers and quickly begins dressing. The woman sits up from a sea of sweat-soaked, mangled bed sheets and rubs her damaged scalp.

"Maybe you should shave your head like the cage fighters do," he chuckles.

"Yeah, … that'd be good for business," she says, rolling her eyes in disgust as she hops out of bed.

"Business!?" he says with a ridiculing laugh.

"What?!"

"No offense but, … I've just had a lot better." The fat redneck flashes a shitty smile and begins draping his large gut with an old flannel shirt.

The woman's body language now becomes a bit more rigid as she slips completely back into her black blouse and assertive but indifferent attitude.

"None taken. That'll be two-fifty."

"Maybe you should just consider this one practice. You know, since you seem like you need it."

"Right after you consider deodorant. That'll be two-fifty," she repeats as she's almost fully clothed.

Annoyed, he grabs his wallet out of his jeans and pulls out three one hundred dollar bills.

"got change?"

"No," she sighs, "I don't."

"Will you be fine with two hundred?"

"No, … I won't. It's two-fifty… like we agreed," she says, slipping her shoes on.

"It's just fifty bucks."

"You're right, so just give me three hundred… I'll be gone and you'll be the one out fifty bucks. No big deal right?"

"Sweetheart… you weren't worth *a dollar fifty*."

"Just give me the money," she says, angrily clenching her jaw muscles.

"Oooh!" The man holds up his hands in a mock defensive

position and laughs.

The woman changes her tone, "Usually I'm better at faking it… but it's just that you were so awful… at fucking. I mean you were *really, really bad*. And you stink, too"

"Better watch your mouth!"

"I feel like I just got raped by a piece of hairy dog shit," she says continuing to verbally batter him while throwing her purse over her shoulder.

"Keep talking like that and I'll give you nothing."

"You don't want to try that," she says with a stern face.

"Oh, really? Why?"

"Just don't."

"What? You gonna fuck me again?" He quips.

"You couldn't pay me enough to fuck your diseased, fat ass again. But what I will do is go back downstairs to your trucker bar and tell all the regulars that you've got the smallest, nastiest dick I've ever seen!!"

The man grits his teeth in anger as they silently stare at each other.

Realizing the man isn't budging, she quickly snatches two of the bills out of his hand. "Fuck it… just fuck it!" she snaps. "Take some of that extra money and buy yourself a bar of soap. Trust me… you need it!"

She turns her back and walks towards the door as the man continues to stare at her.

As she grasps the doorknob to leave, an iron grip on her waist-long hair surprises her as she is violently yanked back into the room. She feels the tearing of her scalp as thousands of little strands get ripped out by the root. She becomes airborne, thrown back on the sloshy waterbed, hitting the headboard and being momentarily dazed.

"YOU THINK YOU CAN FUCKING TALK TO ME LIKE

THAT, YOU FUCKING CUNT!!"

The man pulls the leather belt out from his old, stained Levi's and prepares to thrash her.

"STOP! DON'T FUCKIN' TOUCH . . . FUCK. . .GET . . .OFF!" she screams, turning her back and holding up her thin arms in defense.

With a demon snarl, he starts slashing his belt against her, beating her mercilessly, thrashing her legs, arms and back. Her screams are smothered by the loud, thumping country music mix from below preventing any hope that someone might hear her cries.

The lashing from the leather raises big red and purple whelps on the back of her petite frame. The pain is so intense, her vision fades as she almost loses consciousness. He puts the belt down, rolls her over, positions himself between her legs, and begins to unzip his fly.

"YOU DON'T HAVE TO FAKE IT THIS TIME!" he says with a devilish smile, panting and wheezing in excitement.

Disoriented, she continues to resist by spinning around and sinking her teeth deep into his hairy forearm. He grimaces in pain, grabs her bleached blonde hair, and tries to peel her off of him. His skin stretches from his arm as she remains latched on like a pit bull. They both yell in pain as she pulls up her knees, digs her high heels into his gut and presses the big man off the bed forcing him to fall awkwardly onto the floor. As he begins to get back up, she jumps off the bed and charges him with a whirl-wind of slaps across the face, neck and chest. After this seemingly ineffective attack, the man spins his body back towards her and delivers a crushing blow to the side of her face, hurling her off her feet and into the corner of the room. She is now only semi-conscious. As he begins to approach her, his sadistic smile dissolves into a blank, shocked look. Within seconds his entire face gushes with blood. Long slashes along his forehead, chest and neck open up like a zipper, releasing rivers of the dark red, oxygenated liquid. He drops to his knees as one of his shaky hands reaches up to feel the deep four-inch gash on the side of his neck. Just as his fingers touch the wound, it begins to funnel out copious amounts of his blood down his arm, making his elbow look like a faucet. His eyes roll back into his head and he passes out with his face bouncing like a rubber ball off the wooden floor.

The woman remains on the cold floor, up against the wall, still dazed and bleeding from the blow to her left cheek. Out of breath and full of adrenaline, her chest rises and falls deeply. She stumbles up, legs shaky as a newborn fawn, and steps over the man who is now resting on top of a growing pool of blood. She flips on the lights of the filthy bathroom and looks in the mirror, revealing a little compression cut under her left eye and a small patch of hair missing from her head. Her split cheek continues to trickle blood, adding to her already blood-soaked mouth and teeth. Leaning on the sink to remain upright, she turns on the faucet and splashes cold water on her face, painting the sink with tiny red droplets. She pokes her head out of the bathroom, checking to make sure the man is still on the floor, while dampening a hand rag and wiping her face with it. Light bruising is already beginning to form on her high cheekbones as she looks down, scrubbing the blood off her shaking hands. She turns her palms up to reveal well-positioned razor blades, super glued underneath the bright red, acrylic nails on all but the thumb and forefinger of each hand. Two of them are broken at the tip, making the Freddie Kruger-like weapons even more visible. Each one of the cheap blades is surrounded in gooey, coagulated blood and bits of flesh. She scrubs them, turning the white hand rag into a pinkish color while slightly shredding it.

She hears gurgling sounds coming from the man and sticks

her head out of the bathroom again, confirming that her ene-my is still down. She turns on the sink once more, dampens her hands, and wets her hair, slicking it back to cover the bald patch-es and attempts to adjust her stretched-out, torn black blouse. *"Fucker,"* she says knowing that it's ruined. She takes a deep breath and walks out of the bathroom, habitually turning off the light.

The man's face rests in a pillow of blood and his throat continues to whistle, making blood bubbles as air tries to escape from the wound. She approaches him, picking up his confeder-ate flag-engraved, brown leather wallet from the floor, grabbing out all the cash and glancing at his driver's license. "You owe me a new dress… Jason". She slings his redneck wallet back on his bloody body, puts her purse over her shoulder, and begins to walk out.

She stops, inches away from the door, and turns around. She walks back over to the dying man, lying on his stomach with face stuck to the floor, flips up her skirt, squats slightly, and pisses on his slashed head. "I usually charge extra for this you stupid fuck; consider it a bonus," she says, her lip quivering. She stands, re-adjusts her outfit and walks out of the bedroom, turning off the lights and shutting the door behind her.

The bathtub faucet gushes hot water as the woman's per-fectly manicured, blood-red painted toes grip the knobs, twisting them off. She sinks all the way in, up to her neck in the beige, fiberglass tub and closes her eyes, breathing in the rising steam, warming her cold lungs and letting the hot liquid relax her every muscle. The sound of the drippy sink next to the tub makes her open her eyes and turn her head to stare at every little droplet. She watches it slowly form and dangle on the rim of the faucet until it's heavy enough to crash down against the stainless steel plug, making its distinct "ping" sound.

She's hypnotized by the next expanding droplet as her eyelids become heavy and she begins to doze off. Suddenly a large crash shakes the droplet off. She bolts up in her tub. The crazed redneck slams open the bathroom door with black eyes and an evil snarl, *"YOU'RE MINE, YOU FUCKING CUNT!!!"* he says, rushing at her with his big leather belt buckle.

She jumps awake from her nightmare, out of breath, still in her tub, surrounded by chilly, hours-old, stagnant bath water. The sink still drips. Her bluish lips quiver as each move in the tub causes the cold liquid to stab at her every muscle like a knife. She doesn't move for a moment, her body conquered by terror and cold. She takes in a couple of deep breaths and gets out of the tub, wrapping a white towel high around her chest. She looks into the mirror once more, examining her severely bruised and cut eye. She then moves backwards, closes the lid on the toilet, and sits down, bringing her knees up and hugging them with her arms. Leaning her head forward on her knees, she regains her bearings.

Pop-Tarts shoot out of the toaster as the woman sits nearby letting her fingertips dry from a fresh manicure. She sits on the squishy sofa and sips a hot cup of coffee, using her palms to lift the mug to her mouth while watching Bugs Bunny out-maneuver Elmer Fudd on an ancient, snowy television. She leans over a coffee table with a clear package of cheap, red acrylic nails and a box of Exacto-knife blade replacements. A small super glue lid hides behind her big coffee mug as she carefully puts a small line of the adhesive on the inside of her left ring fingernail and then slowly sticks the blade vertically along the glue line. She blows on it a little and sips on her coffee once more.

She walks to the bedroom and opens up her closet. Taking a beautiful dark, red dress from a hanger, she rips off the Macy's price tag and drapes it over her shoulders, slips on strappy, silver high heels, and finishes her make-up, expertly avoiding her armed fingernails. She then slings a black leather purse over her shoulder, looks into her full-length mirror, and makes small adjustments. The cut under her left eye now hides, barely noticeable, under the thick make-up. Taking a deep breath, she puts her shoulders back and walks out.

The woman is making out with a clean-cut, black man in the booth of a dimly lit nightclub. The place is winding down as people in matching aprons move around, cleaning and putting the chairs on the tables, wrapping up what is the end of a private party. The man is growing more assertive with his kisses, moving down her neck and beginning to touch her breasts. She grabs his big hands and stops him.

"Hey, hey . . . slowdown a little, baby." She says with a smile.

"I'm sorry," he says, pulling back a bit. "I'm just... I'm having a great time," he says coming back to kiss her, his breath laden with alcohol.

"The party doesn't have to stop," she says stuffing his advance once more. "We can go all night. But... we need to talk business."

The man's love struck and toothy smile dissolves as he pulls his hand out of her grip. He begins to act a bit awkward, adjusting his posture, sitting up straight and creating some distance.

"Oh... Oh baby, she says sensing his discomfort. "I thought you knew what this was about. I'm sorry," she says sincerely.

"No... Don't apologize," he says looking down acting a bit embarrassed. "I know exactly what this is about. You're just... really good. That's all." He flashes a shy but charming white smile, "You almost had me fooled." He shakes his finger at her and swigs the last bit of his watered-down scotch.

A bit of pity escapes her expression. "I'm really sorry, David. It was so nice meeting you," she says with a respectful smile as she starts to climb out of the booth. The man grabs her hand and pulls her back in the booth.

"Wait! . . . Don't go," he says with lonely eyes and a desperate voice. "What can I get for two-fifty?"

A Love Trumping Lust

The lust flows through my veins, married and mixed with the red liquid that keeps me alive. I want to believe that I can control it, that this primal sin that infects my dreams and thoughts can be defeated with discipline and self control, but I know that it can't be because with every heartbeat, with every breath it saturates me to the point where I can taste it in my mouth while it conquers my mind effortlessly.

The sight of you sickens me more every time I am in your presence. Your beautiful body, your symmetrical face and your sweet scent, as sweet as the scent of devil-grown, forbidden fruit, intoxicates me and stiffens my body's softness, shaking me uncontrollably.

Your voice fuels the flame of my desire for you and even though you say, "no", to me, your voice boils the lust that poisons my blood, manipulates my thinking and tells me that you want me.

I know that you only want to be friends and I know that your heart belongs to another. A part of me –the good part– wants to be happy for you; it wants you to live the life that you want; it loves you enough to let you go, but that is not the real me. You don't understand that the goodness residing in me, that is willing to let you go, is only a small part and that the thimble-size amount that I have is dominated by something that is possessing me more and more each day, something I couldn't possibly control - something I don't *want* to control anymore. The majority of what conquers me is a side you've never been able to see. The passiveness and friendliness you trust is nothing more than a show that, to this day, I wonder why I keep presenting to you, my only audience member.

I don't know why I keep going back to you, seeing you and talking to you and smelling you. I don't know why I torture myself by having to touch you friendly when touching you friendly aches me. But I'm forced to see you. I'm forced to trust the beast inside me who drives me to you. He talks to me. He tells me things I don't want to believe, things he's tried for years to convince me on, and only now has he actually become convincing. He tells me that you taste even better than you smell. He tells me that you would taste even better if you were scared, that your goose bumps would tickle my tongue, and that your frightful shakes would make your muscles weaker and your legs easier to spread.

He tells me that you really don't know what you want, that the man you love is a false prophet, someone whose seed is of poor quality because his soul reeks of a putrid decayed quality, not of a real man but of a pseudo-man: a wimp who would rather kiss on your cheek but not really taste you; who would want to make love to you, not fuck you; a man who would put a condom on without asking, instead of coming deep inside you without asking. A man who would need you, but not lust for you, someone who would love you, but not worship you.

The wicked one inside of me tells me it's okay if you put up a fight because your lips will taste better with a little blood on them and that the clothes you wear will tear like thin tissue paper off your skinny body. He tells me that deep down your trembling, natural frailty secretly craves the lustful violence that I could provide.

I believe him. I want to force you, I want to fuck you, and I want to wipe that look you give me off your face: the look of friendship, of safety and of trust. I want you to uncover the monster that painfully claws inside me wanting to get out, wanting to get to you. I want to see you tremble and cry and scream. I want you to look at my face with shock knowing that the friend you once saw in me is no longer there. I want to taste your salty fear and acquaint you with the real me: the demon that gives me the power to make you moan in pain, fear and pleasure all at once, the black soul whose lust is a virus, an infection, one that will turn you from a victim, to a begging whore with just a flick of my tongue and transform you into a slutty vixen who's willing to let me take you over and over again because you'll finally see that light without darkness is artificial and hollow, and the sinful pleasures of the blackness always bring about your greatest fantasies, because it's a place with no rules, no taboos, a place where your desires attack you, a place absent of god or judgment.

The other whom you feel is the one for you - he is gone. I cut his throat and stood over him as I watched his moral blood spray from his wound and onto my pant leg, and I looked down on his death and smiled. I told him I would take care of you and he cried with his last breath. Tomorrow you'll get the news and you'll drop to your knees in pain, but I'll be there to catch you. You'll wrap your skinny arms around me at the funeral and you'll cry and scream and ask me how someone could do such a thing. I'll hear you but won't answer, because your scent will once again boil my blood and your body heat will tempt me with the hot meal that I crave so badly.

You'll be wounded and weak needing a friend and wanting me beside you. I'll be there like I planned and I'll be good until it happens. It'll be you that does it. You'll make the first dangerous move and you won't even know it. In a desperate time, you'll reach out and kiss me on the lips. For the first time in years, you'll display a singular act of affection that shows itself as more than friendship. You'll release a wave of lust in yourself that you didn't know even existed. You'll tell me to stop but I won't, and you'll hate me for doing this to you, and you'll hate yourself even more for liking it. You'll taste my seed and want more because the lust that I have for you saturates my body and spikes my fluids, making your ego bloom like a rose in spring. And when you look down and see that your pussy is my heroin, you'll gasp and, at that moment, fall in love with me. And then you'll realize that the lust that I have for you has trumped any love that you've ever experienced.

The next morning, you'll wake a stranger up from your bed and toss beside me the large hunting knife you found on the night stand, the one still caked with the blood of your lover. You'll ask this stranger, with tears rolling down your face, "Why did you do it?"

And I'll smile and say, "For you, baby... I did it for you."

Killers

Tears roll down the face of a little girl as she stands in the middle of a busy aisle in a Wal-Mart super center. She screams, her stressed, water-logged eyes desperately searching for any hope of familiarity. A large, clean-cut man kneels down.

"What's the matter, sweetie? You lost?"

She nods her head up and down while clasping onto her dirty stuffed teddy.

"Well, come with me. I'll help you find Mommy," he says, grasping onto her little hand and guiding her towards the front of the store.

"Oh my god!" a young woman says, sprinting across the store and kneeling down to embrace her daughter.

"We were just looking for you," the man says with a friendly smile.

"My god, honey, you scared Mommy," she says panicked and out of breath, her relief quickly turning into anger as she begins to casually scorn her daughter.

She makes eye contact with the tall man and rises off her knees while holding onto her little girl in a tight bear hug.

"Thank you so much!!"

"Don't worry about it."

"I took my eyes off of her for a second and… she was just gone," the young mother says with a sigh, while subconsciously pushing her daughter's bangs out of her eyes.

"Well, it's easy to do this time of year but she was in no

danger. We found you."

"Well, God bless you," she says giving the stranger a quick, shy hug.

"You too! ... And Merry Christmas," The man laughs.

"Merry Christmas to you!" she says as she walks away and continues to lecture her daughter.

The man smiles and shakes his head while drifting back off into one of the aisles.

The man adjusts his scarf against the cold and walks out of the busy store, holding a few plastic bags with his leather-coated hands, his hot breath clashing against the cold, dry December weather, smoking the air. Christmas music plays in the background as the man approaches a guy wearing red and waving a bell.

"Merry Christmas, sir," an old black man says to the tall stranger in passing as he puts several dollars into a Salvation Army's red bucket.

"Merry Christmas to you," the tall man says in return as he walks out to find his car in the busy, hustling parking lot.

He walks past rows of cars, dodging and moving around the creeping automobiles that circle the front of the store like vultures, looking for the perfect parking spots. He continues walking until the crowd of vehicles diminishes. He digs for his keys in the pocket of his grey wool coat, pulls them out, and hits the remote button, unlocking a freshly waxed, sleek-looking Mercedes. He throws the bags in the back and hops in the seat, making the cold leather interior squeak with each little shift of his body. He pulls out of the store parking lot, clicking his headlights on and hits the nearest onramp, jetting down the dark icy highway.

"Yeah... yeah baby, I hate these all nighters too, but we have got the mortgage to pay," he says, talking into a pricey cell phone.

"I know, I know. I love you, too. I'll call you on my way home. Give the kids a kiss for me." He flips closed the cover on his silver cell phone and cruises down the highway while scanning the radio stations. The radio lands on a Christmas channel and he exits the highway on an abandoned, streetlight-free road. He flips on his brights and turns off-road, driving in through a wooded area.

"Oh, the weather outside is frightful, … dum … du … dum," he sings while his body bounces in his seat.

Tree branches thump, scratch, and hit the perfect paint job as he continues driving, the rough terrain bottoming his Mercedes every few feet.

"Let it snow, let it snow," he sings as he slows down, looking around a section in the woods that is unusually treeless.

"Yeah, this is it." He says to himself as he brings the Mercedes to a complete stop, pulling the emergency brake lever towards him and getting out of the car. He opens up the back seat and pulls out several pieces of firewood and throws them in a pile on the cold ground. He reaches in and grabs a full box of matches and can of lighter fluid.

The bright flames reflect off the man's eyes as he stares into his big, roaring fire. His grey wool coat is off and his colorful Christmas tie hangs loose around his neck as he chugs on a bottle of Jack, occasionally spewing a spit of it onto the fire. He stretches his arms, looks at his watch, and slowly walks over to his car, a bit tipsy. The black Mercedes, now slightly scratched on the sides, reflects the fire like a mirror as he opens the door to the back seat and pulls out the rest of his bags, placing them on an unfolded cloth on the hood of the car. He pulls out items from the plastic bag and from the back seat: a worn out Louisville, a shovel, two glow sticks, some brown shoe strings and a big roll of silver duct tape. He walks around to the trunk and pulls out his keys. He opens it, and the bright fire illuminates the dark trunk, revealing a bound, half-beaten, young girl. She's asleep, her duct-taped hands resting up against her face. Her feet are bound with the tape as well, wrapped up all the way to the knees. He grabs her by the feet and arms, picks her up out of the trunk, and drops her onto the frozen ground. The girl, awakened by the crushing feeling of air rushing out of her body, rolls over in pain, her mouth opened wide trying desperately to refill her lungs.

"Rise and shine," he says kneeling down to her. Her face distorts with pain as he looks over her with a smile.

"Come on, wake up. You need to wake up for this, sweetie," he says, retrieving the baseball bat leaning up against the car and walking back over to her.

"This always seems to be the worst part," he says with a sadistic smile. She looks up at him in shock and, without any warning, he swings the baseball bat with all his might and slams it into her left leg, breaking it like a thin tree branch. She screams so loud that it causes the man to squint his eyes as the shriek appears to wake up the whole forest.

"Girl, you've got some lungs on you," he says, tossing the bat on the ground and sticking his fingers in his ears.

She rolls around, withering in pain.

"Sorry. I just had to do that… if I undo all your tape, I can't be chasing you all over the woods. Bad knee you see," he says as he pulls out a serrated, folding knife from his pocket and begins to saw away on her tape, cutting her legs and arms free. Her cries begin to decrease, her body trembling. She vomits profusely, causing her to cry harder as the remnants of her last meal shine on her chin.

"Don't worry. That's just your body going into shock. It means your knee will stop hurting soon," he says as he walks over to the car and pulls out a thick quilt and spreads it on the ground by the fire.

"Get on the blanket," the man demands as he returns to the Mercedes. The girl starts crying again, looking up at the man with pleading eyes.

"Get on the blanket," he says more firmly as he turns his head over his shoulder and begins digging through the trunk.

She just cries harder.

He turns around, runs over to her, and begins to kick her.

"YOU STUPID LITTLE CUNT ... YOU ... DO ... WHAT ... I ... TELL ... YOU ... TO ... DO!!!!" he says, kicking her hard between every word, forcing her to crawl onto the quilt.

"Now, take off your clothes!" he says as he walks off.

She looks at him, confused.

He walks ten or fifteen feet from the campsite looking for something, his Mag brand flashlight a bouncing bright ball on the ground. He slips backwards and falls into a big, pre-dug hole.

"Oh, uh," he says climbing out. He turns around and opens the wrappers of two glow sticks, snapping them and throwing them in, lighting up the little grave. He returns to the campsite and sees the girl off the blanket, desperately trying to crawl on her hands and knees to nowhere. He runs over to her, grabs her by her pants, and launches her airborne. She lands on the blanket but bounces off, nearly landing in the fire.

"YOU FUCKING BITCH! DO I LOOK LIKE YOUR MOM-MY? HUH? NOW TAKE OFF YOUR FUCKING CLOTHES OR YOU'RE GOING TO BE A FUCKING LOG FOR THAT FIRE! DO YOU HEAR ME?!!"

The young girl starts to plead for her life, but not with him. Grasping onto her broken leg, she pulls her knees together and begins to pray.

"Please, God……. please!" she says, her eyes bleeding tears while looking up at the crystal clear, dark sky, the stars twinkling like Christmas lights.

He laughs a little and looks up with her towards the starry black sky.

"Sorry, sweetie, I don't think He hears you," he says as his eyes turn from the stars and lock back onto hers.

She finally takes her sights off the heavens and faces her demise as he slowly starts to approach her. Despite her young age, the young girl senses death coming as her body begins to shake again.

Suddenly the man comes to an abrupt stop, freezing where he stands, the cold air crystallizing his muscles. He stares forward in shock, his sinister smile melting like ice on July asphalt. The young girl immediately turns, looking around her shoulder, and sees three men wrapped up in camouflage, all holding high-powered hunting rifles. Their warm breath rolls out of their mouths like steam engines as the girl gasps in disbelief and, with all her might, crawls over to the man in the middle, latching onto his leg like a life preserver. The hunter looks down at the girl as she starts crying and trembling up against his leg. He then looks up at the tall stranger.

"I….. I was trying to get her some help…." He stutters.

"Shut up," one of the hunters snaps, his deep, resonating voice carrying with it the scary sting of a predator.

The middle hunter pries the girl off his leg, takes his thick camouflage jacket off, wrapping her up in it, and picks her off the cold ground. He looks at his other fellow hunters.

"We'll meet up with you," the other's say to him as he takes a head start and walks away with the girl, disappearing into the woods.

"Ok, I . . . I think you guys are confused," the tall stranger says with a shaky voice, his Christmas tie hanging loose around his neck and the cold air giving away his increased, smoky respiration.

The hunters both laugh as the shorter, stockier one grasps onto a bone grip hunting knife, unsheathing it from its leather holster. The shiny metallic blade lights up, copying the bright firelight.

The other hunter picks up the Louisville slugger and grips it tight, his knuckles popping.

"Well, I wish we could talk more but…. we got up extra early so we could, you know, have a better chance to get that kill."

The tall stranger stares back at him in panic and begins shaking, his eyes filling with tears.

"And since we ran into you and all, it's . . . well, it's kind of screwed up our plans. So….. I think you owe us something."

The tall stranger's Adam's apple ripples in his throat as he gulps at the large hunter creeping up, blocking the flames and casting a shadow over him. The man doesn't try to run. He only falls to his knees and begins to cry.

The hunters walk out of the woods, the middle one still holding onto the injured girl. Emerging light begins to slowly kill the dark shadows that once conquered the forest as the awakening sun casts morning light over the men and the girl, warming her cheeks waking her up. The girl looks up at the bearded stranger as he charges through the woods: the harsh, cruel outdoors unnoticeable to him. She doesn't know who they are or where they are taking her, but she feels no fear. She knows this killer is her salvation.

One of the hunters stops and kneels by a thawing river stream. He dips his blood-caked hands and hunting knife in the crystal clear water, bathing them clean. In the horizon, the outline of a large extended-cab pickup truck appears as the men slowly push through the bitter wind to their destination.

Primal

Bright hall lights illuminate the floors and walls of the dark room as the creaky apartment door swings open wildly, causing the doorknob to dent the cheap sheetrock. The large man enters and then slams the door shut, returning the blackness. He shuffles around the lightlessness with wet shoes and a thick damp coat, his breathing erratic and loud. The clicking of a switch on a small table lamp sounds loud in the quiet efficiency as the tall, gangly, white man plops down on the big leather couch and hunches over grasping onto his hand. His wet hair rains water droplets onto the old hardwood floor. His face scrunches up in agony as subtle moaning sounds escape his clenched jaw and pursed lips. He looks down at the blood-drenched rag wrapped tightly around his hand, so saturated that it has begun to form big, fat crimson drops, detaching and spattering onto the scuffed wooden floor with his every movement.

A tuxedo-colored cat comes over to comfort his owner, purring and rubbing on his leg while lapping at the growing pond of blood between his feet. The man pets the cat and stands up, taking off his thick, green jacket and carefully pulling his injured hand out of the sleeve. The collar to his white t-shirt is stretched out enough to fit around his waist as he uses the bottom of it to blot and dab on the nasty-looking scratches on the side of his face. He limps across the room and flips on the light in a small, white, tiled bathroom.

The man looks into the mirror, turns on the faucet, and

scoops up some water with his good hand, splashing it on his pale, pasty skin. He takes a deep breath and starts to unravel the now red-soaked towel from his hand. He puts his bloody appendage in the sink and watches the water slowly wash off the wound, revealing a mangled, severed index finger. He gasps loudly, staring at the grayish bone peeking out the top of the meat stub snapped at the end, like a broken pencil. He twitches and puts his hand over his mouth, then quickly aims at the toilet with his eyes, drops to his knees, and vomits until he has nothing left but drooled gags. He exhaustedly flips the toilet lid down and rests his bloody cheek on the side, catching his breath. Still on his knees, he reaches over and opens the under-sink cabinet and removes a large first aid kit. He sets it in front of him and flips open the tin lid with one hand. He stops and closes his eyes for a moments' rest using the toilet seat as a pillow and then, when he's ready, begins to pull out the contents of the kit.

The hot water faucet fills the tub with dancing, bubbling liquid. The air thickens with steam as the man turns the knob off with his large, gnarled hands just in the nick of time before it spills over the edge. He opens up a window to allow the air to clear out and eases his whole naked body into the smoky water.

The man's hand is bandaged with almost professional quality, and a couple of big globs of greasy antibiotic ointment remain smeared over his facial wounds. He relaxes for a moment and starts to close his eyes only to be awakened by the tuxedo cat whining at him, proudly displaying a dead mouse lying on the tile floor. With little emotion, he stares at the cat's green, carnal eyes and blood-stained mouth. The cat's meows act as a lullaby as he drifts off to sleep.

The sun's rays invade a little window over the kitchen sink, shooting light into the cramped rundown apartment. The man stands in the kitchen and fills the cat's food bowl with a big bag of off-brand, dry kitty food, overflowing it and making it spill onto the floor. The cat eats what's on the floor first. The man then rolls up the empty bag and sets it on top of the fridge.

The resonating voice of a male morning news anchor drones on about the week's upcoming weather out of an old, box-style television. The man continues buttoning a blue vest with a "Gino's Auto" logo while glancing at the news. He opens up the cupboard, puts a bowl in his mouth, and then crams a big box of cereal and milk in his good hand. He walks over to the kitchen bar, sits down on a tall, rotating stool, and pours his cereal and milk, scooping up the food with his good hand.

The television flashes a "breaking news" graphic behind him as he eats. The sound of the male anchor's loud, dark voice blares through the apartment.

"Channel 2 news is first to bring you this amazing tale of survival. It happened last night, around 2:00 AM, downtown on the corner of second and Delaware."

The statement immediately grabs the man's attention as he straightens up in his stool and his posture stiffens.

"A young woman was attacked in her apartment by a man in an apparent rape attempt."

The man slows his chewing and clenches his jaw muscles, but continues to look forward not turning to the television screen.

"According to police, the woman was somehow able to severely injure her attacker and escape by running to a nearby fire department, where she was taken to the hospital and treated for minor injuries. Local authorities currently have no leads but have linked this to several other sexual assault/robberies that have occurred in this area. If you have any information please call crime stoppers at 1-800-Crimestoppers."

The man display's no emotion and goes back to his cereal. The tuxedo cat bulls its way to try to get into his food. The man shoes him away. "Get!!" The cat comes right back.

"GET!!"

The cat stands away for a second, but simply cannot resist the drops of milk the man loses onto the table as he tries to spoon his cereal with his left hand and comes back.

The man explodes, smacking the cat making it fly across the kitchen and onto the floor hard. The cat hisses at him, terrified.

"YOU FUCKING CAT!!" he says as he throws his cereal bowl at the tuxedo kitty covering the yellow kitchen walls with milk and raisin bran.

The cat dodges the cereal bowl, hops on the counter, and hides behind the microwave hissing. With a deranged look, the man darts from behind the counter and reaches back behind the microwave grabbing at the cat, but the feline balls-up on his arm and sinks its teeth into his flesh. The man jerks back and clasps onto to his hand as the cat runs under a small kitchen table.

"FUCK!!" The man says, clenching onto his now bleeding forearm. He grabs a kitchen knife and corners the cat. He reaches around and scruffs the tiny kitty from behind the neck, picks him up, and holds the knife painfully with his bad hand just centimeters from the kitty's throat. The cat still hisses at him as he once again looks into his green eyes becoming almost hypnotized by them. The man's face begins to relax as his flared nostrils start to shrink and his teeth hide back behind his lips. He calms down and releases the cat, throws the kitchen knife in the sink, and leans on the counter, breathing deeply. He opens up the medicine cabinet, grabs a bottle of aspirin, pops the top, and takes down four pills, crunching them without water. The cat stands just out of reach in the doorway of the kitchen watching him. The cat then approaches him and rubs against his leg in forgiveness. He stops and looks down at the cat, rolls his neck, and then puts on the thick green jacket that was draped over the chair, a scarf and a big winter hat. He then throws a gym bag over his shoulder, kicks off the lights, opens the door to a bright, windy day, and shuts it behind him.

A cast of light creeps over the pitch-black apartment floor as the door opens, engulfing the dark room slowly but illuminating it fully like an artificial sunset. The light then dissipates quickly as he shuts and locks it behind him. The man walks across the room, clicks on the end table light, and takes off his jacket. He plops down in the big leather couch and looks around for his cat that is usually there to greet him. He kisses and calls for the cat.

"Here Cat!" he says, making kissing sounds with his mouth, but he receives no response. He gets up and walks around the house, checks the back rooms, and finally the bathroom.

"Shit!" he says, realizing that he had left the bathroom window cracked open.

He opens it up fully, sticks his head out in the cold, rainy weather, and looks down three stories to an alleyway. He sees nothing but the wet, shiny black streets. Panicked, he throws on his jacket and exits the apartment.

He walks down the dark, quiet alleyway hunched over and cold, with his hands in his pockets calling out for his cat, almost in tears. He looks across the street and under a bright alley light, to his disbelief, he sees his tuxedo cat rummaging through a dumpster.

"OH!!" he says out loud, a sigh of relief overcoming the man as he runs up the street calling for his cat, which looks up at him, starts meowing and walks towards him. He turns towards his kitty, but without warning an old model Lincoln Town Car blasts through the alleyway. The cat hits the side of the car, bouncing off the windshield and falls to the street. The man is hit in the shoulder by the passenger side mirror and is thrown to the ground. The car screeches to a stop as red brake lights reflect the glassy streets. Without any concern for his own injury, the man slowly gets up and hobbles over to his cat. He strokes his battered pet, but it barely moves and musters up only enough strength to let out a small whimper. A large, big-bellied man steps out of the car and walks up several feet behind him.

"Jesus Christ!! Are you all right? You know what time it is?! Huh?! What are you doing sulking around a dark alley like this? Do you hear me you dumb shit?"

The man looks at his cat and starts shaking it, ignoring the man.

"Hey man... I'll call you an ambulance but I ain't paying for this. You walked right in front of my car," The driver says pulling out a cell phone. "In fact... screw this. I'm calling my lawyer first."

The man looks up, his nostrils open wide and his face distorted.

"Dumb asses like you need a license to walk!!!" The driver grunts.

The man stands up, reaches in his pocket, and flips open a four-inch hook knife. He walks up to the man on the phone.

The driver puts his cell in his pocket and looks up at him

The man slashes him across the throat with lightning speed. The driver stands motionless for a moment looking back at him in shock. He takes a few steps back and coughs a little before his throat suddenly turns into a blood sprinkler, spewing and spitting everywhere as the big-bellied man falls forward on to the dark, wet pavement.

The doors kick open in an emergency animal hospital.

"HELP!!!! ... I NEED SOME HELP!!!!!." the man screams, holding his half-dead kitty in his jacket and bawling like a little boy.

Two staff members greet him and try to calm the hysterical and clearly mentally unstable man down.

"Sir! You need to calm down right now!" says one doctor, grabbing him by the lapel as the other staff member scoops the cat up and runs down the hall.

"What?!" the man says not paying attention and looking over the doctor's shoulder at his kitty.

"Sir... just take a deep breath. Sir? You need to relax! You are scaring people!"

Out of breath and crying, the man looks around the room. The other patients stare back, gripping their pets tightly. He searches for an empty bench and walks over, sits down, and buries his face in his bandaged hands, still crying. That evening's head staff member looks at the man from the other side of the reception desk, walks over, and begins to comfort him.

The dingy living room lightens up as the door is nudged open by the man's foot; his hands are full of groceries and a large pet taxi. He shuffles across the room, clicks the light on, and drops the groceries to the floor, but carefully places the pet carrier on the edge of the sofa and opens it up. He looks in and smiles while exhaling loudly and leaning back allowing himself to sink deeply into the sofa.

The man sets a plate of food on the kitchen table and lights a pretty red Christmas candle. He runs over to the stove and retrieves two tuna fillets off a sizzling grill. He plops them on a plate and, chopping them up, blows on them to cool them down. He walks over to the other end of the table where his heavily bandaged, immobile cat lies in a little kitty bed he has set up. The man puts the plate of freshly cooked tuna by the cat that lifts its head up, takes a few sniffs, and begins to eat it heartily.

"Careful... it's hot." The man says with a big smile as he

watches the cat chow down. He picks up his fork and begins eating dinner as well, the bright candle and the small oven light acting like beacons, the only lights in a dark apartment.

A Monster by Association

When a child is born, you either make the commitment to love them unconditionally or you don't. Of course, upon their birth, you may blurt out that you do, but so does every parent. They say that they love their child, no matter what and that there's nothing in this world their kids could do that would change that. But just saying it doesn't mean it.

People don't look at me like I'm human anymore. They haven't seen a human in me for the last ten years; they have only seen a monster in me. Why? Because I refuse to break a promise that I made so long ago and I am simply unable to extinguish a love that many think I should.

Let me ask you something: do you love your child? I mean *really* love them? Do you tell them every day that you love them more than anything in this world, including yourself and that you'll never stop loving them no matter what? *"No matter what"* is quite a loaded statement, more than you know? So really think about it for a moment. You've gotta use your imagination to make *sure* you're not just fooling yourself and saying shit that could someday come back and bite you in the ass. You can't just look at that innocent little baby propped up on your lap right now looking at you with big eyes and pure love. That's too easy. You've got to do better than that. You got to picture them older, all grown up trying to make it in this world, but you got to stop picturing them graduating from medical or law school, all happy and successful and perfect, while smiling and waving their diploma and holding up your equally perfect grandchild. You see, that's not reality; that's just your own little fantasy playing out in your mind.

How about if your kid will instead just go through school like you did: not stupid, but not particularly smart either, just average. They, like you, might be good enough to get into that community college across the street where they'll go for two semesters and then drop out, because life just got in the way. Like you, they'll get a dead-end job making $11.50 an hour for the rest of their life. Then they'll get married to an annoying person that you'll want to think isn't good enough for them, but deep down, you know they're just right for each other. They'll pop out two kids and then they will just start to get old, occasionally calling you in tears asking to borrow money for mortgage. How about that? Still love them? Of course you do. This is reality, right, not some fucking sitcom and you know that. Life is hard. It was hard for you and it isn't going to be any kinder on your offspring, but it doesn't matter because their your kids and you still love them, even though they didn't live up to their full potential, or worse, that they did and this – community college dropout, $11.50 an hour with two kids, is it.

It's okay though; they are good people, a good father, mother, whatever. Your children don't have to be mega successful for you to be proud of them and love them. After all, you're not only down-to-earth but you've always considered yourself a smart parent. You preached birth control to your children because you knew that teenagers have sex and that abstinence is a joke. You let them have alcohol at your house underage as long as they didn't drive because you're a realist. You went to bed those nights feeling so smart and not like all those other bible-waving, head-in-the-clouds, dumbass parents next door whose kids were pregnant even before they got out of high school. Perhaps your son or daughter will come to you one day in tears telling you that they're gay, but your extreme open-mindedness trumped any awkwardness or worry, so you hugged them and everything was fine. Again you went to bed that night feeling great about yourself because you're not some closed-minded redneck; your love is solid, concrete, and dependable no matter what.

You're different, you're enlightened and you meant what you said when you held them in your arms when they were still gooey from the womb and told them with tear-filled eyes that you would love them forever, but you never truly tested yourself because, to do that you've got to let your mind go places it doesn't want to. I know it's hard, but for a moment don't picture your child as just another underachiever; those are a dime a dozen and easy to love. And don't picture them as just some "hell raiser" with a couple of misdemeanors on their record because they got bored on a Friday night and took down some mailboxes in your freshly waxed Lincoln Town car. You're taking the easy way out.

Here... let me help you. Close your eyes for a moment and picture your child something much worse than just an awkward loser. Imagine them being seemingly normal, happy and healthy. See them being all those things you wanted them to be. They love you and they show it. They hug you every time they see you. They kiss you on the cheek and look in your eyes with those same baby eyes they did when they were crawling, and they tell you

"Dad, Mom, I love you. If you need anything..." and you go about your life proud that your kid turned out alright. They turned out to be someone great. They have money and success and it's all because of them but at least partly because of your great parenting... or so you think.

Then, one day, just before your sixtieth birthday, you get a knock on the door. It's a police detective and he's here to tell you some bad news. You immediately assume he's there to tell you that your kid has been murdered or hurt, but that's not it at all. Your kid is alive and well—they're ok, but before you can enjoy that momentary sigh of relief, the cop has other news. This stranger—this jerk of a cop—is sitting in your living room at 2:00AM in the morning trying to tell you that there is another side to your kid: a dark, horrible side. You don't believe him of course, but he still tries to convince you that he knows your kid better than you. You get so angry that you'd punch him in the face if it weren't for that badge he was wearing, but before you can tell him to leave, he's got more news.

This is the part when you might be thinking I discover that my kid has killed someone—that, in a fit of rage, they have done something crazy and has ruined their life forever but that's not it. There's more to the story. What my kid did had nothing to do with anger or rage; instead it had more to do with desire: a deep unquenchable need to feed this thing inside them, this awful thing that I didn't even know existed and now challenges whether or not loving my kid is still morally sound.

But before I tell you what my child did, you have to pretend you don't know yet. Pretend it's your kid and someone has come to your door telling you that they're a monster but doesn't have the heart to tell you exactly why.

Remember, it's "no matter what," right? So it wouldn't matter if I told you they killed someone and not only did they kill someone but they didn't stop with that someone. They planned and organized it, like they did the first time and, with cold-blooded premeditation, your kid did it again… and again… and again… and again… and well, you get the point. Your baby likes taking lives. We're a long ways away from that boring underachiever by now and we're about to get even further, but it doesn't matter to you because, even though your kid took some lives in cold blood, you still love them, right? Even though, there are now dozens of devastated and broken-hearted families in their wake? You don't approve, you don't think what they did was right, but you stand by them.

Ok… but what if you were to find out your son didn't just kill them? What if you were to find out your little angel enjoys and actually gets aroused when they see someone in pain and I'm not talking dominatrix-get-you-off pain, I'm talking about raping someone after they'd cut their victim's throat and enjoying the sound of their victims coughing, choking and dying, like a sweet lullaby to their ears, or discovering that burning people with a hot iron and making their victims scream are the only things that can make your child orgasm.

Tough shit to swallow but it gets worse. In fact, what if you were to find out that the only way your kid can even sleep soundly at night is by knowing that the trophies they kept from each of their victims are close by, safely wrapped in plastic and tucked in various spots in his basement, the same basement you helped clean out when their family moved in ten years ago.

Hell, it just seems like yesterday that you and your wife took their family out to Red Lobster and you ate and laughed and had a great time because you saw that your wonderful son wasn't depressed or sad anymore. He was happy, he was living his life to the fullest and that made you happy. Little did you know your kid was happy that night because when he went home, he went down into the basement and tortured, raped and murdered some innocent victim they had waiting for them in a homemade cage. The food that you bought him was still in his belly when he killed someone that night, but still….. You love them, right?

You'd go visit him in jail, willing to sell everything you own for the best defense attorney in town, but it's too late; there is no defense. He did it. He confessed. His hands began to shake and he starts crying out loud to you, grabbing and latching onto you like he used to when he was just 2 years old. Now he screams and cries and tells you that he's sorry and that he's sick and that he needs your help and his pain, his fear, they're not fake, they're sincere because you *know* him, he is *your* child; *you* know when he is really faking. But it doesn't matter because everyone else looks at him as a monster because he *is* a monster. What are you supposed to do? Relatives, very close ones, are all now turning their backs on him, and as soon as they hear details of the horrors he administered, they cut ties immediately. The very mention of his name makes people cry. Your baby has no one else; he's all alone. Even your wife, his own mother can't face him.

So, would you still love them? Love them enough to still pack them treats, cigarettes and food, anything that you can find in the house and mail it to him every day so they'll have enough shit to trade and bribe their way out of prison beatings. Would you still be committed enough to go every single week for the next ten years to a maximum security prison to hug and kiss and hold your little monster and tell them that there's nothing in the world that they could do that would stop you from loving them?

I made my decision years ago, to stand by my son and be with him until the end even if that makes me a monster too. Would you do the same? Would you still love your kid if you found out, like me, that they had killed in cold blood? Would you still call them your "son" or "daughter" if they didn't stop with just one? Could you still kiss them and hold them if you knew they didn't just kill them, but purposely made their last few hours on Earth a living Hell? Could you still look him in the eye and tell them that you forgive them and that you still love them no matter what and that you will continue to keep loving them to the end and beyond? Forever? Even if you knew the worst, that the oldest of all the victims they killed and tortured in that little basement of theirs was only seven years old? Could you? Knowing full well that standing by your *child killer* wouldn't change who they were, wouldn't repair the pain they had caused, and wouldn't do anything but simply make you a monster, just *by* association.

So think about it. Would you do the "right" thing and turn your back on your kid or would you do the "wrong" thing and continue being a loving father or a loving mother because that's what you promised to that little baby on your lap, all those years ago; that's what you promised yourself and deep down that's what you still owe them, because, as I believe, it was *you* that brought them into this world and right or wrong, it is *you* who should stand beside them, unconditionally. Can you tell yourself honestly that despite this, you would still love your child or will your mind just go in denial and keep repeating, *My child would never do that.* Ten years ago I would have said the same thing...

I had a dream. I was still waiting for you, waiting to see the person that you would grow up to be one day. They say you're blessed and I believe it, but blessed by whom? You're smart, handsome and perfect, but it's your very perfection that frightens me. The flawlessness with which you perform things is your only blemish because it singles you out and pushes you far away from the very definition of human. Despite your youth, you radiate a unique calmness that can turn any room silent and your indestructible fortitude allows you to walk this world completely unshaken, free of any fear or uncertainty about your future. As a young child, you acted as if your destiny had already been prepared and you carried with you the confidence that only ancient wisdom could provide.

Every parent before me has hoped their children would grow up right, with a moral purity that would bring about goodness. I am no different. I prayed for this benevolence as well, but I often found myself pondering, *What if you're not good? What then?* Would God demand my bond with you be broken, my love for you be extinguished? To me, committing oneself to love only a moral child would show a devotion with limits and mine has none, not for you.

I had a dream last night. It was of you. You were all grown up: so smart, strong, beautiful and handsome, just like I had imagined, but you weren't what I thought you'd be. I saw your perfection manifest into a phenomenal power, an incredible force that exploded into something that couldn't be controlled. I watched your strength become a virus that plagued the weak and struck fear in all that was good in this world. I saw you use your intelligence to destroy human morality and I watched you reinvent it to your liking.

I heard your voice; it was as dark as sin and as powerful as armies. It spoke destruction but when it sounded, millions listened. You were up on a pedestal. The skies around you were stormy and in creepy chaos and with the clouds gathering, the wind whirling and the lightning crashing, the very sound of your voice shook the heavens and made the angels cringe. The people were afraid of these black skies as they represented an inevitable doom, so they flocked to you like frightened cattle looking for an escape from lightning, for salvation; yet they didn't see it, they didn't know that it was you who had blackened the very skies they fear.

I saw you up there, declaring war on your enemies and I saw your adversaries crumbling with just a point of your finger and you celebrated with screams of victory, your sinister smile devoid of any pity. And the hellish blaze of war and suffering followed you everywhere. Not as a fearful glimpse of your eternal doom, but rather the very color you were destined to wear. Only the frightful, grayish shades of charred earth, wreaking with the stench of cooked misery and death are the only things that freed people from your trance, allowing them a brief glimpse into a soul so sinister that they could only wish you were completely devoid of one, but you are not; you are darkness worse than the void that would have been without the creation of light. Like the monsters that you were told didn't exist, but whose eyes glowed over you from your closet at night, your evil is pure and it is real, uncontaminated by second guesses and without a trace of self doubt or personal torment; for the horror that you have brought upon humanity has made the very mention of your name a sound of terror. You have long since crossed that invisible line and walked so many miles past it, the very demons who came before you, who dropped mankind to their knees in your wake, tremble in your presence, for their darkness looks as bright as the sun next to you.

And in the midst of this mayhem, I see myself beside you and I'm not unhappy; I'm not ashamed of you and I haven't abandoned you. Instead I am proud. My love for you has long since poisoned and killed any other values or beliefs that would have ever opposed you. This is because I know in my heart that your only true weakness is me. I know that I am the only one who could ever halt your wicked reign that is your legacy. But I don't and instead, I sinfully embrace the very unique destiny that I have conceived into this world. Every innocent life you take and every drop of pain you administer is justified in my mind without a second thought because you are my child. You are my everything to me. And I rode alongside your deranged soul through that life and into the next, no matter where it goes, for Heaven without you would be my Hell, and Hell with you would be an everlasting salvation, a cool breeze across the heat and despair of our desperate humanity.

In my dream, my morality was a blank canvas, a fresh piece of clay that I placed in your hands. My very soul's destiny and the side that I chose… was waiting for you.

No matter what, right?

Better This Way

When I would feel myself in the shower, I'd close my eyes and imagine it was you because it was always better that way. I loved it all, from how you would wrap your dainty little hands around me and strangle me to the breaking point, to how your lips always felt cool amidst the hot water. It was always so perfect when we were together. We would make out like teenagers in the steamy bathroom, kissing each other until our lips were numb, and then I would pick you up and carry you to the bed, your skin as hot as the water from the shower when I dragged my tongue across your soaking wet body. You would giggle and adjust your legs telling me, "That tickles" with a smile on your face that begged, *Come kiss me again.* You wouldn't avoid my scarred face and would instead kiss it over and over again, loving the very thing I was most insecure about. And when you let me enter you, your eyes would close and you would lean back, extending and exposing your neck displaying a trust that only those you love ever got the privilege to taste with their eyes. And your body was as warm and as wet and inviting as the shower.

When I would sit alone in my little apartment and the quietness would become painful, I would close my eyes and pretend you were there because it was always better that way. We'd order pizza and you would laugh at the cheese sticking to my chin. We would watch TV on my cheap, old box set and make wisecracks at some crappy video rental that we got and your laughter was so loud it would put life back into my mind. We would sleep through the night without moving once and wake up late, the warm noon air opening up our eyes to a beautiful day, and even though it was always you who would awake in my arms, it was me that felt so wrapped with love. We'd go to the park and you would hold my hand in public, tightly without letting go once, and a sense of pride would come over me, knowing that you: this beautiful, smart, perfect person was proud that I was yours. Then we would go out to dinner and indulge in fine wine and fatty foods and share dreams with each other that we both knew, deep down inside could never happen, but it didn't matter because we had each other.

When I would lie on my couch sleepy and alone, I would close my eyes and pretend that I was stroking your hair as you slept across my lap. It was always better that way because, you see, you were the best thing that ever happened to me. But I fucked it all up tonight. I made a judgment call and I was wrong. I wanted to be normal. I saw you every day. I talked to you every day, but you didn't know me. I wanted to walk up to you as you sipped your coffee and ask you out for steaks and wine, but I couldn't—I just couldn't. I would tell myself every single day that today would be the day, but everyday another day came and went. You were always so beautiful and surrounded by tall, handsome people who were as charming and as pretty as a sunny day. But despite this, you had this look that you deserved someone, not only better than them, but something that even perfection couldn't provide. Something I knew I could never give you.

I have thought about the justification for my actions and I assure you, deep down, they were innocent. I always felt that you would know that we were meant for each other the moment our lips first met, even if, up until that very moment it was forced upon you. I felt that, if I could pull this off, my imagination would come to life and for the first time, I could close my eyes and then open them and you would still be there. But that didn't happen.

When I crawled into your window, I expected for you to leave with me willingly. When I snuck up on you sleeping, I expected your fight to be short and something that would be followed by an apology and a "thank you," but instead reality massacred what we had. When I grabbed you, you screamed in terror. When I kissed you on the lips, you felt nothing but a stranger and you lunged, beat on my chest, and clawed at me with all your heart. I didn't want to fight back. I didn't want to hurt you, but when I looked down, you were already bleeding and you were hurt badly. I didn't even know what I did. I always told myself that I would kill any fool who ever tried to hurt you, but when I stopped for a moment, just to pause and see what I had done to the love of my life, to my soul mate, I felt a heavy object slam across my face. I fell to the floor only to get up because I wanted to see who did it; who hit me across my face and opened up my scars. That's when I looked up and by the window with the bright moonlit night, I saw that it was you, standing there trembling and injured, holding a revolver in one hand and a night lamp in the other. It was you... *you* did it; you hit me in the face, you hurt me. You were screaming at me not to move, but I didn't listen. I meant you no harm. I just... I just needed to hug you. I had to tell you I was sorry for hurting you. I had to wipe the blood from your face and to kiss you, I had to ask for forgiveness, and if you would have given it to me, I swear I would have crawled out the window I came in and left you alone forever, keeping with me just your memory. But instead your forgiveness came in the form of a bullet. I felt it go through my chest before I heard the gun go off. It hurt, but not as bad as the sight of the relief on your face as you stood there over my dying body.

I know you're scared and if I could talk, I would tell you that everything is going to be all right. I know you're already poised and ready with that silver revolver of yours, to put another round in my chest if I recover, but if I could speak, I'd tell you to relax and stop crying because I'm not going to recover. If I could, I would tell you that I'm sorry for hurting you, sorry for scaring you, but my lungs, they're filling up with the blood from my torn heart.

I know our reality wasn't a good one and as I looked into your tearful eyes with in my last moments, I truly wish you could have stepped into my mind and swam in my fantasy for just a single day to see how happy we could have been together. But you won't and instead you'll forever remember me as the creepy guy behind the coffee counter who handed you your morning coffee: that quiet, shy guy with a scarred face who couldn't look at you in your eyes and always seemed so sad to you.

But it's ok… it's ok because over the years, I have grown accustomed to reality's cold truth, and as I extend my hand out and reach for yours with my last breath, you just give me a cold nervous stare, it is at this moment the truth as to what I am and what you see me as is finally revealed to me, for in the midst of my lethal utopia of love and hope and you, the sickness that has clouded my mind all my life has finally cleared and for this brief moment in time, I understand that I am in fact that lonely, disturbed and dangerous person that everyone has told me I was. *I am* that person that never deserved you.

But as I close my eyes and begin to die alone on the cold floor, I'm going to take your memory with me. I imagine you coming over and gripping my hand tightly while stroking my hair and looking into my eyes while slowly easing me into a peaceful death. It might not be reality and I might not deserve it, but… it's better this way.

Deicide 6

de•i•cide *n.*(ˈdi ə ˌsaɪd)
1. a person who kills a god.
2. the act of killing a god.

Tonight as you cast down your hand, I will lay scorch to your precious heavens and the people will look upon it in awe and smile as you tumble to your disgrace. Your delight for carnage will die with your word, and I will strip from you the power to judge what shouldn't be and it will only be then that you will remember my name. For, dear Heavenly Father, tonight I pray that when you fall… you fall all the way.

A young father sponges his child's back in a grey soapy tub, the purity of the child's blond hair still imminent even though darkened by the soak. The father looks on, his face stoned with a love that poisons him numb and freezes his gaze.

"Dada!" the child says proudly, smashing two bath toys together squeezing their sog out and onto his father's pant leg. The warm water deludes the toxin that stupors him, and he snaps back smiling at his boy while moving to the side his waterlogged bangs away from his big brown eyes.

"I love you so much," he says to the three-year-old that smiles back at him clueless to love's density and returns to his colorful toys. The young father reaches in to kiss him, soaking his white button shirt transparent.

"Do you love daddy too?" The father says with a smile, trying to wedge his face between the child's focus and his toys, but the boy has grown tired of his father's obsession.

"Hey, … Do? You? Love daddy?" the father says again as the child

resists, flashing an ornery smile.

"Say it!" The father says, torturing him under the water with a thigh tickle. The kid shrieks with laughter but doesn't give in.

"Say it!" The father continues until the child's stubbornness depletes from the bracing exhaustion.

"I love dada!" he says like a chore but with a genuine smile.

The father laughs and kisses his soggy head.

The old, grey-haired man sits up from his bed and hunches over the edge with his forearms resting on his thighs. He sighs from the rise of another day and looks out the open bedroom window absent of its usual early morning glow. He gets up, close to the wood-framed bay and watches the heavy winds spit the parked cars outside with moisture.

Once fully clothed, the old man walks out onto his balcony and watches the last of a valiant morning shine illuminate the dark overcast of the glowing grey. In the horizon, the piercing sunlight stabs the grimy sky through, touching the land with a few shimmering rays of hope, but these rays are only short-lived as the agitated gale seeks out the bright foothold and fills the hole, darkening the land below once more. The old man, sipping coffee and leaning up against a post, looks on with the calm and peace of a soldier, a tenacious spirit resting before battle. He stares at the wind chimes in chaos, clinking together like anger-possessed steel, whose tinging sounds gather in the air and stack onto each other creating an almost constant ring behind the colliding beat of the hollow metals slamming each other, as the angry breeze molests the man's morning comb over.

With your every taunt know that I grow calmer. So continue to taint me with your bullying breeze that stinks of doom and rejoice in your coward-ice. Hide behind your darkened blanket… and be thankful that I can't see you.

The young father lies on the littered hardwood flooring, his body broken from the gusty throw. His dirty blond hair sponges up the bloody gash, keeping the wound from bleeding in his face. The inside of his house is now outside as the open-roofed dwelling shines bright doom and debris and the winds rage so hard they pin him down and sling papers and books at him at damaging speed. He flexes hard, lifting his head up to see his child lying in the bathtub, older but only by one first missing tooth.

"Dada!!!!" he screams.

The father flexes with all his heart to try to get up but is thrown back down. The child screams in terror.

"CLOSE YOUR EYES!!!!" the young man yells.

The child continues to cry as his father's words are lost in the wind.

"CLOSE YOUR EYES!!!!!" the father repeats with all his firmness making a prayer shape with his two hands clasped.

The child shakes his head, clinging onto his teddy. The father gets up to his feet and holds onto a still-standing house frame.

"CLOSE YOUR EYES!!!" he repeats, demanding his son to borrow his fealty.

The child looks at his daddy one more time with trust and finally does what he says, burying his little face in prayer hands. The father smiles and begins to fight the winds and get up to him.

The deafening explosion of a transformer drops the father to his knees, making him grab his ears from the percussion. He grasps hold of one of his eyes and yells in pain from a piece of shrapnel that makes it bleed out through the pits of his fingers. He stares with blurry single vision at his kid in the tub trembling but still not looking, locked in faith's flex. A small red car hurtles through the air as if weightless and smashes into the bathtub before another gust of wind picks up the father and slings him into the still-erect bricked fire mantle.

The old white-haired man awakes in a sweat, surrounded by holographic weather pattern images that float atop a glowing

table. He wipes the sweat and looks out the window at a sixty
-mile-an-hour spring-green blurry view and senses a change in
the direction.

"I said head north," he says, standing up and pouring some
strong coffee this time with one hand and rubbing his eyes with
the other.

"Major rotation two miles due south," the tall gangly young
man says while manipulating the graphics floating all around
him with artistic flair: expanding, reducing and creating colorful
images that bring the storm onto the table in a digital light that
looks more than real.

The old man responds sternly, "There's major rotation
north."

"That's not the one," the tech says nervously.

"Not the one," the old man repeats with a scoffing edge.

"Nothing out there ta chew on 'cept cattle," the kid replies.

"And if it turns?"

"She's a no go, professor."

"And if she turns?" the old man repeats.

"So what if it does? It's too far out," he says pulling up the
graphics as they both look. "She's a big, tough girl... but she's
peaked early. She's terminal."

The old man says nothing but communicates his message
with a doubtful gaze, his pursed, irritated lips about to burst open
as his tongue rolls across his teeth, his patented warning.

The tech sighs through a frustrating smile. "She's been
sputtering since she was born... this is the one..." the tech says
pulling up another small but growing cyclone, "You want your
clearance? There's your clearance."

The old man looks and gets closer. He looks at the graphics and then looks back at the table. He slowly wraps his hand
around the tornado image, squeezing it, smudging the colors,

"She looks healthy."

"She's double tough," the tech says, confident of his decision.

He takes his glasses off and rubs the stress from his eyes, "Meaks… we got one shot… .We got one shot to show the…"

"This is it," Meaks says, interrupting his doubt.

The old man looks at him hard and clenches his jaw in concern.

The gang of Jeeps, trucks and motor homes display sci-fi curves as their polished paint shimmers against every bright flicker of the sky that does nothing except growl dooming anticipation. While the vehicles are kept well clear, their coats begin to bead the solitary raindrops that fall from the sky uncoupled and alone. They ride in a tight group, heading down a vacant highway towards the black clouds ahead. They keep going until they leave the road behind and continue off-road and down the fielded pasture.

Inside the back of the truck, the passengers all surround the image of the rotation that has expanded over the projection table.

"One mile across and growing," Meaks says while decreasing the size of the image and including the makings of a small suburb that seems to be in its path.

"Refresh it for me," the old man says, popping his knuckles and lacing his boots.

"She's on a kill path… Nothing but warm flats and all the two-bed one-baths she can eat," Meaks says with a serious tone.

"We got an EF4 here, guys," a female computer tech yells from the back.

The professor breathes nervously while putting on his jacket and equipment.

"It's projected to reach the center of Edmond area in twelve minutes," Meaks announces over the speaker of the ten or so computer techs in the other trucks.

The professor looks at him and then looks back shaking his head slowly and with confidence. "I don't think so... make sure the bosses are getting this data," he says to Meaks, who has been calling it in all along.

"He's gonna give us the go... isn't he..." Meaks asks with an anticipating smile.

"Just stay on her..." the old professor says patting the young tech on the back and walking outside.

The convoy of trucks pulls up to a flat field as the men and women exit their vehicles eager to confront their enemy. The massive cyclone almost blackens the entire horizon as the old man looks at the deadly funnel—not with fear, but with a hatred of a demon, letting his nostrils flare out and taking in the gust of wind, savoring the smell of his adversary.

"The monsters!" the young child cries, pointing at the closet.

"Monsters?" the young father says, pointing at the closet.

"Get em... get em!"

"Over here... in here?" the father says clenching his fist, making the kid giggle. The father shakes the clothes and creates an epic mock battle in the closet.

"You... leave... my... boy... alone!" he yells timing the words with his punches making the child clap in satisfaction.

"Ok... all dead," he says walking back up to the child's bed.

"No....eat em!"

The father sighs. "Oh yeah... forgot," he says going back to the closet and pretending to eat the imaginary monster corpses.

"Mmm," he says.

"Monsters tasty?" the kid asks.

"Yummy!" the father laughs.

"Give me some!"

"You want some monster?" the young father says, walking over and giving him a piece of nothing that he pretends to munch.

"Mmm…"

"Tasty?" the father asks.

"Tasty," the kid confirms.

"Next time you can just pray that the monsters go away. See? Look!" he says closing his eyes, "Dear God, please eat the monsters."

"I want Dada do it."

"Yeah, but It's faster if you do it this way. Just close your eyes and …"

The kid interrupts him by sticking his tongue out and blowing, and the father retaliates with a barrage of tickles that the kid tries to fend off with little hands.

"You like it when Dada does it?"

The kid nods.

"Well… we'll only do it that way if there's a monster daddy can't handle, Okay?" the father says adjusting his son's pillow. "Lucky for you, there aren't many monsters that Dada can't handle," he says tucking in his boy's sheets.

"Watch Dada! Dada gonna get em!" the child says grappling with the air.

"Oh Yeah!"

"You gonna eat green noodles… and then you go ARRR!!" as the child punches his imagination.

"Mm hm… Green beans make Daddy strong," the father says displaying his biceps.

"Get back, Monsters! Stop hurting people, Monsters!"

The father leans in and kisses him, "Hey…." he says.

"Go back in the water monsters!" the kid says, continuing with his attack.

"Hey…" The father repeats, finally getting the kid's attention with his

eyes, "Go to bed."

"Dada stay here!"

"Dada will always be here."

"Sleep here?"

"Dada sleeps in his own bed."

"One... one time," *the kid says extending for a hug.*

"You got two minutes," *he says snuggling with his boy, who wraps his father like a teddy.*

The father starts to snore real hard on purpose, tickling his side, and the kid shrieks in laughter and looks at his father as if he were God.

"Sir!" one of the college kids yells, the front of his crimson ball cap reading: UNIVERSITY OF OKLAHOMA METEORO-LOGICAL SCIENCES, the top covered under his raincoat while he grasps on with both hands trying to keep the hood covering him from the stout, bullying winds. The professor continues to look on, trapped in a determined stare at the massive cyclone, forty or so safe miles out. The rains begin to cut sideways and spray right in his eyes and drip off the reflective safety goggles that drape around his throat like a necklace.

"Sir!" he repeats louder, attempting to get the professor's attention.

"Sir!!"

"What!!!" the old man says, annoyed.

"Sir... You got it... Sir, you got your green light!! Birds' all just left Tinker!" he says shouting real close to his ear.

"Huh?" the professor says, looking at him with disbelief at the arrival of a moment that he's been waiting so long for.

"Come on... got front row seats to history," the guy says, yelling every word as he pats the old man on the back and heads in.

"Ok," the professor says quietly while staring back at the tornado.

"Come on, Doc…"

That's good news…" the professor says with a fixated stare as he begins to ramble quietly to himself.

"Hey… let's go snag some dry," the big kid says with concern.

"I'm gonna get a closer look," the old man says, walking forward towards the spring-green fields of long grass that goes on forever, meeting the sinister horizon ahead as it sways and flows against the cyclonic chaos like a green ocean.

"We're good!" he yells at the kid.

"We're what?" the big kid yells back with a shrug.

"We're good… we're all good…" he keeps repeating with his eyes fixed on his target.

"ETA's 1 minute, John!!!" the kid says extending his arms in question, clueless to what the professor means.

The old man just keeps walking forward now—a little faster.

"Hey? … Hey!!!" he hollers seeing the old man's deaf walk towards the storm.

Ignoring the boy, the old man continues to look up at the torrent sky with a smile as his walk turns to a light jog.

He slowly strokes his son's hair as he sleeps on his chest.

The professor's communication device activates as Meaks' voice comes through the static.

"Hey, Doc… We're all set," Meaks says, talking through a small blinking ear piece in the professor's ear.

"We're good… We're good!" the professor says, mouth breathing heavily.

"Yeah… yeah, we're all good here… Hey… where you goin'?" Meaks says with a confused smile from inside the mobile base headquarters that rocks back and forth against the winds like a boat floating in the rough.

"Just… keep… just keep the line clear," the old man says

breathing with old, lab-rotted lungs, his eyes beginning to glass up.

He laughs a little, "Yeah... Okay... But? What'ya doin?" Meaks asks.

"Just... keep ... keep 'em open," the old man says, choppy and out of breath, as he raises his shaking fist to his mouth and bites it.

"What?" Meaks says with raised brows as everyone in the tech station turns to the young tech with questioning eyes.

"Just keep 'em open... Just keep 'em open... !" he says as his words struggle even more to emerge from his lips, having to wrestle through the beginnings of a trembling voice.

"Hey man... listen why don't we um... Why don't we start you headin' back?" Meaks says his smile now gone over the wireless frequency.

"He wants... he wants me... I have to do it.... I have to do it ...I have to do...!" he says, repeating each word with an absence of sanity while beginning to cry like a child and wheezing, his speech incoherent as he searches the skies all around him with his eyes.

Meaks looks around at the staring and concerned staff. He nods his head towards the rest of the team as they all give him a moment of silence and listen to the tormenting song of a father's agony as it comes through the speakers and fills the back of the truck.

"John?" Meaks says calmly.

"I have to do it...I have to..." he says, now crying with a draining pain that sends shivers.

Meaks then mutes the audio feed to the room, giving only him communication.

"Go get 'em, Dada," he says quietly to the professor before terminating the line.

The professor takes the earpiece communication device out

of his ear and rips off the goggles from around his neck as his jog now turns into a full sprint, wheezing and crying the entire way.

He looks down at the well-dressed body of his son placed nicely in the shiny opened oak casket. He looks down with a look of hurt that sickens even himself.

Reaching maximum capacity, his sprint slows as he cries with the deep moaning mourn of a terminal sufferer.

The minister looks up from the floor with his nose smashed and bloody as two large men flex with all their might against the young professor as he screams with the snarls of a demon's worst nightmare, kicking and lunging and punching at anything holy or within arm's reach.

The professor mumbles his words whistling and riding his wheeze out as he falls to his knees from pure exhaustion.

He looks up as his nemesis, the almighty enemy and his machine of destruction, and for a moment is caught in the awe of its massive presence causing him to tremble a bit, his hate not immuning him from the fear. His eyes flood as he bows his head in a moment of helplessness.

As his palms lie on the ground, they begin to feel an intense vibration, like a quake that becomes rattling. He takes some gulps and looks back up at his enemy, this time not with awe but with a hatred that could split atoms.

"Open your eyes, son," the old man says in a whisper, like a prayer.

The sound of a sonic boom deafens his ears, allowing him the pleasure to know one has made it. That's all he needs to hear as a car-sized aerial pod jets past him towards the great tornado, blasting right into the heart of it with the fearless charge of the secular steel that reads: NDDT-DEICIDE 6 on its side. The old man holds his revengeful rage as the aerial pod is followed up by another, and then another, before an entire grouping of ten, fifteen and finally twenty pods fill the skies as the swarm of his ge-

nius invades the black funnel and he watches as the robotic creatures change form, ejecting wings allowing them to be picked up
in the rotation, giving off nothing more than a bright red blinker
as they ride the winds upwards. The great tornado continues to
suck up the poisonous shrapnel as the cyclone swirls like a Christmas tree, displaying its cancer-like sparking tree lights. The father
watches as the blinkers begin to pulsate quickly and then explode
in a flash of light.

The father looks on with naked eyes where he lets the bright
light rupture his sight red, ignoring the temptation to blink and
choosing instead to savor every second of his delivered wrath,
one that heals his wounds, as he watches his dehydrated enemy,
now nothing more than a funnel-shaped cloud stripped of its
deadly fertility.

The people in the control room hug and clap and celebrate
as the powerless twister rains down its deadly carry of shrapnel along the horizon, while the heavy chemical-enriched clouds
melt and fall from the sky.

The professor looks down and closes his eyes, letting a
bloody tear leave his damaged sight and roll down his cheeks.
He stands up slowly, the humble victor. In the distance, several
students rush to his aid.

A Kiss' Bliss

The forty-something's reflection shows more years than truth as the chubby man dressed in a white button-up shirt parts his hair to the left, combing a thin layer of blond hair over a red, sunburned bald spot. His blue, tired eyes sit on plump shelves and tell stories of sleepless nights and a calloused spirit as he pins a nametag over his left pocket that reads: CAL METZ - STORE MANAGER

--

"You don't really look like a burger joint kind a gal," Cal says to the brunette who sits across from him and seductively works her malt up a thick straw with gentle sucks, teasing him with flirty smiles and blood-red lips that wrap around the thick vanilla ice cream-filled straw like a noose around a neck.

"I'm more of a Cal kind a gal," she says back with an irresistible grin.

"Hmm. . . That'll be a first" he says with a chuckle, momentarily breaking his eye contact with happy embarrassment.

"I'm also a vegan."

"A vegan?"

She nods.

"You know... there's milk in that *milk*shake."

"Whoops" she says unapologetically as she pulls the malted straw out of the lid and licks it clean while not breaking eye contact.

He gulps as he watches her pink tongue run along the shaft.

"What's with them?" she says, looking past Cal and flashing back a shitty smile at the crew of burger joint employees who are gawking at her with distrust from behind a counter.

He turns around to see what has piqued her interest.

"Find something to do," he says to his team, making them scatter, before returning his attention back to the brunette.

"Seems like a friendly group," she says sarcastically.

"I wouldn't say friendly…. more like… colorful."

"Colorful?"

"Yeah…colorful………They're just wondering why *you're* talking to me."

"Why wouldn't I talk to you?"

"Because they know, I don't got any money," he says with a slight head tilt before taking a sip of his afternoon coffee, "If we keep this up, they're liable to think that I got hidden talents or something."

She smiles big.

"I could go over there right now and tell 'em about your freakishly big dick," she says with a shrug.

"Could you say it with a straight face?" he says, making her laugh. "Besides I'd hate to disappoint."

--

Cal swirls a red tie under his collar, effortlessly creating a Windsor knot without looking. He smiles as he puts his jacket on, and it aches his reflection with an unfamiliar mold.

--

Her long legs wrap around his big belly, barely making it as she fucks him from atop like she loves everything about him, with all her heart and all her body holding nothing of herself back, giving him her everything as he lies his head back with heavy eyelids and a gaping mouth, intoxicated by her fuck, giving him more than he ever deserved to have.

--

This will be your store someday. You'll get a crappy company car, a shitty raise, and a lot more responsibility," he says, taking off a greasy, sweaty white button-up shirt and putting another one on in his office. "And best of all… you'll smell like onions no matter how much you bathe. Interested?" he says, making the black girl smile.

--

"Tomorrow then?"

" Yeah," he says looking at her, completely love struck.

"Eleven thirtyish?"

"Yeah."

"You'll be alone?"

He nods his head.

She kisses him while sitting on his lap. She gets his tie and straightens it up for him as his happiness blooms. He gives her a store key that hangs from a chain necklace. She looks at it.

"Don't tell anyone… my employees don't even get a key."

She looks at the perfectly engraved numbers across the key head, and the 'Do Not Duplicate' stamped in metal and runs her finger across it.

"Those numbers, that's the alarm code, so you don't forget."

She looks at him as if it was the most beautiful jewelry she'd ever seen and kisses him.

--

He gets into his car and sets a silver-wrapped little present in the passenger seat before pulling his grey civic out of the garage and driving off.

--

"THREE DOUBLE CHEESE, MUSTARD, NO MAYO, FIVE LARGE FRY… MEDIUM VANILLA TO GO!!…" The short, round, black fry cook blasts as she goes down the line in a frantic pace unhooking baskets of frozen fries and dunking them into large vats of grease, her hands moving like a serpent's tongue, working the fryer as if it was her destiny.

"TEN IN DRIVE THRU AND STACKIN! LET'S SMOKE IT UP IN HERE!!" she screams again as a tall, tattooed blonde, who looks tougher than pretty, hits a button on the iPod deck making the rhythmic sounds of the band FOSTER THE PEOPLE blare out the Helena beat and fill the Burger Street burger stop with rhythmic pop sounds. Another tall black man works the grill like a pro, flipping down fifteen or so red patties, seasoning and re-flipping the smoking and browning meat with a custom spatula that he made himself, maneuvering the burgers with a certain finesse, twirling it around his hand masterfully as if it was an ancient weapon of the patty forged by a lifetime of practice. The metal on the cooking utensil sparkles against the morning sun and reflects a golden plaque on the wall that says URBAN EATS BEST '09, '10, '11, '12

Cal stands with his hands crossed as he looks over at his handpicked top-notch crew, grinning with the pride of a coach who is certain that he's got a winning team. The black girl puts a couple of large cups under two dispensers right next to Cal and turns on the chocolate shaker, filling the 32-ouncers rapidly just before walking away. Without looking Cal turns them off by a quick elbow at the perfect moment before another worker scoops them up and lids them. Cars line up in the drive thru all the way out to the street as the tattooed blonde dances seductively as she brings milk shakes and grease-stained bags of burgers out to the cars, making old fat men smile with glee as she pinches one on the cheeks. Meanwhile Cal slices open a big box and dumps the contents onto a silver counter, sending a wave of ketchup and mustard packets sliding across the slick surface.

A small-statured man with a cap that sits low on his head tries to fit more twenty-dollar bills into the front slot of the floor safe, using a spatula to cram down the loads of cash that already have piled up on the inside and stack right up to the opening, making it almost impossible to add more.

--

Cal stares at a wall filled with framed newspaper clippings:

"LOCAL BURGER STREET STORE #56 TOP EARNER IN THE NATION FOR FIVE CONSECUTIVE YEARS" the headline says, displaying a black-and-white picture of Cal, who stands with his arms crossed in front of his four-person team of burger pros.

"LOCAL FAVORITE LEGENDARY SERVICE" another article is titled.

"7th CONSECUTIVE STATE STORE MANAGER OF THE YEAR" says the first article.

--

The grill man throws cheese, tomato and onion slices with scary accuracy on the still-sizzling burger before grabbing a yellow and red bottle and spinning the condiments in his hand with just the flickering of his fingers, making them break dance with balance on his palms before halting their spin with a firm grip and delivering rapid-fire quarter-sized dollops on each patty, all with identical quantity. They work with rhythm and skill, communicating without the need for words with each other

--

"I'm outta here, baby," the new girl says to an exhausted Cal, who is abruptly awakened from his desk. "You comin'?"

"No," he says reaching in the drawer of his desk and popping the lid off an Aspirin bottle before crunching a couple of pills without water, his face distorting from the bitterness.

"You got plans or somethin'?"

He nods his head.

"So I heard," the black woman says, folding her arms.

"So you heard what?" he says rubbing his eyes.

"Heard you got plans."

"Then why'd you ask?" he says beginning to yawn.

"No reason… Night, boss," she says as she walks away.

--

The key slowly enters into the slot and turns as a gloved hand opens the store. The brunette walks in and Cal comes out of the darkness, surprising her and making her jump and squeal with laughter. He locks the door behind her and arms the alarm before scooping her up and taking her to the back.

"I got something for you," he says.

The remains of what was the perfectly-wrapped silver present litter his desk as new diamond earrings dangle from her earlobes and a couple of empty glasses coated with scotch surround a half-full bottle of Jimmy Walker. She makes out with him, straddling his lap, her curves and ass one of perfect youthful symmetry as her gorgeous body contrasts his overweight, pale appearance. But she kisses him like she wants him and kisses him like she loves him, poisoning his mind with so much disbelief and happiness that just the feel of her lips makes him drunk with joy. She looks him in the eyes as she kisses him, her dark browns showing a passion that he thinks couldn't possibly be faked.

"If it seems too good to be true… it always is… right? Who told me that?" the black, heavyset lady says to him as she leans against the doorway and watches Cal put his jacket over a salmon-colored shirt.

He smiles a little.

"Do me a favor, would you, Flory? Forget everything I ever told you," he says as he bathes his neck with a bottle of brut cologne.

He walks up to her as they share a spot in the doorway. "I'm not kidding," he says as he grabs her hand and gently squeezes it.

"You're way too sharp to be taking advice from someone like me," he says before releasing her hand and walking down the hall.

He breaks away and looks at her hard, staring at her beautiful blood-red lips that have smeared and colored the corner of her mouth. She smiles at him, displaying snow-white teeth, and he smiles back before kissing her again one last time.

"It ain't real... it can't be... you know that," Flory says to him as he walks out the door.

He turns around and shakes his head.

"I'm done with real." He says looking at her with eyes absent of logic and filled with love.

The sound of the locked front door chimes open, making their passionate kiss freeze in time. He pulls away and looks at her hard as she displays an odd, sobering expression of guilt as he gives her a numb gawk of intoxicated confusion. They share a moment of what seems like forever, not saying a word, but him screaming at her with just a silent stare. Finally Cal lets out a painful gasp and gulps as his drunken bare emotions bubble to the surface, making his eyes begin to glass up ready to burst, forcing her eyes to do the same.

He begins to try to turn around.

She stops him by hugging him tightly.

"Don't," she says with a whisper in his ear before barely pulling back and gazing in his eyes closely. Cal looks at her with big wounded saucers, while feeling an undeniable presence behind him.

She shakes her head. "It'll be easier if you don't," she says with kindness. "Just look at me."

"Easier?" he responds, his lips quivering with a nervous grin, the surging hurtful feelings of betrayal numbing Cal to the touch.

"Shh…" she says, putting her finger over his mouth.

"I…I think I have to leave… It's time for me to leave." he says, nodding his head, trying to get up.

"Cal, listen to me," she says, interrupting his incoherent ramble and keeping him firmly in his chair.

His eyes dance around before pursing his lips and shaking his head.

She grabs both sides of his face firmly.

"Baby what we have…. it doesn't have to end," she says, pleading to persuade him with her eyes.

"I can't… I got…. I… just need to go ok…"

"Kiss Me," she says with a grin.

He hesitates, hypnotized by her gaze, his breathing very heavy and rich with spirits.

"I got to go," he says again with a prayer-like tone, his lit eyes still love struck, as they get lost in her dark irises.

"I know you do baby… Kiss me…"

He looks at her beauty with admiration while running his fingers through her hair.

"Kiss me and I'll make it feel real forever. I promise," she says with a genuine smile and a firm nod, as a few remorseful tears run down her cheeks, becoming colored with her mascara.

He wipes the dark drops off her face with his thumbs, smearing her complexion a runny blue. He kisses her with all of his heart and she kisses him back, keeping her promise.

--

The four men gather around the fifth one as he uses a blow-torch, burning through the floor safe. The brunette sits on a chair staring past them, her arms, neck and face spattered in blood. The sound of a metal chunk hitting the ground snaps her out of her daze. The men whoop and holler with joy as they open up a floor vault filled to the brim with twenties, fifties and hundreds.

With a handful of the copied keys, she aims them at the old mop bucket that sits in the corner, and using the wall as a backboard, she makes them each plop into the grey dirty water.

"It's like a fuckin' bank opened a burger joint!" one of the five says as they pull out a couple of large duffels and empty the large floor safe still full from the lunch and dinner holiday weekend rush.

The alpha of the group, a tall, longhaired man, smiles at her and throws her a handkerchief as he walks up.

She catches it with blood-soaked hands and looks back at him with an expressionless face as she pulls her wig off revealing her matted dishwater-blond hair underneath.

"Same story, different town. Right?" He says looking down on her while gently patting her on the cheek. She looks up at him with fearful respect, nodding as he walks away.

She throws the last key in the bucket and pulls her earrings out, setting them down on the desk. She looks at the freshly copied key Cal gave her that wraps around her neck by the necklace and fingers the grooves before tucking it back into her blouse.

A black van pulls out and leaves the restaurant.

Cal's old model grey civic remains in the vacant parking lot.

Red Skies

When I was a little boy I often dreamed of beautiful, rose-red skies and would awake to blue ones, disappointed. I grew up in a world where the human race woke up every single day and walked an impossibly thin line, just one slip away from total extinction. My parents told me that I had a great, great grandfather who worked on the first atomic bomb, the one used to destroy Hiroshima. He was a scientist who emigrated from Germany. His life's work, along with several others, was to create something that would change human history forever. I wonder what he would have thought about me: his great, great grandson's whose life's work would end up being to stop his.

I, like so many in my family, was blessed with a mind full of thoughts and ideas, a brain that saw things differently. This allowed me to discover science, my first love, at a very early age. As our relationship grew, so did my confidence. Every time I put on my bright white lab coat, my destiny became a little clearer. Unfortunately, despite my prodigious abilities, most of what my mind thought up didn't play out in reality. My young life had been riddled with disappointment and failure. If only the real world could be as beautiful and as magical as my imagination.

Out of all the failed experiments and disappointments of my career, I finally stumbled on one idea that was in fact pure genius and could not only survive outside the sanctity of my mind, but flourish in a place that had, up until this point, been my greatest enemy: reality.

My idea was simple: to produce a nuclear explosion. Uranium is required to produce a nuclear explosion. Without it, fission, or the splitting of atoms, cannot occur. Whereas uranium 238 is abundant, in order to make a nuclear weapon, it must be purified to absolute perfection, making uranium 235. With 235, it only takes about 9 pounds of uranium to make a bomb. And since it is the fission that creates the force, it must not contain the slightest of contamination; otherwise a nuclear reaction would be impossible. It's the fission that creates the force. Even other bombs, such as the hydrogen bomb, that use the properties of fusion in their explosion, can only do so as a result of generating fission. This means, that even in fusion bombs, fission must occur to generate the explosion.

This is when I created Reddium. Reddium is a molecularly engineered dust that, when blown by the thousands of metric tons into the air, can create an artificial atmospheric mist. Entire cities can be saturated with this engineered mist in less than a day. It's not a good thing. Reddium is toxic to humans and it can block sunlight, giving the atmosphere a reddish hue, creating a Martian-like sky. The silver lining though is that it also makes entire cities completely toxic to the atmospheric purity needed for a uranium fission explosion. Reddium does not stop the atoms from splitting; it just decays the uranium, weakening the structural membranes of the surrounding atoms, actually making the atoms easier to split but dramatically reducing the destructive force once it does, in essence choking the bomb at the moment of detonation. This weakening of the atomic membranes prevents the atomic chain reaction and makes nuclear warfare an impossibility on any city saturated with my creation. It also turns out that Reddium is extremely easy to produce in mass quantities and it readily dissipates into dirt and sand chemistry after several days, causing no measurable damage to the environment. The first tests of Reddium were done on November 2, 2050 on an island off the coast of Australia. It was funded by a private anti- war company that was set up shortly after the destruction of Israel, the Sinai and the Gaza strip in 2042.

See, though I was born in the United States, I never considered myself an American. My self-love and my grandiose egotism were always too great of a burden for the flag of one country to bear. So I labeled myself a humanist rather than an American, hoping in part that this would increase my fame, distinction and potential for wealth in an increasingly globalized world. I also knew that a defensive anti- weapon of this magnitude, if given to just one country, even my own, would become nothing more than an instigator for aggression. So, seeing the entire world as my market, on that fateful fall day in early November, I created the greatest leap backwards in the history of weapons technology.

As I live-cast the experiment, nations big and small, from every corner of the world, watched me instantly reduce what was once considered the most devastating and threatening weapon ever created to a force no more formidable than a dozen sticks of dynamite, generating barely enough energy to destroy a small truck. As my ego had predicted through all those lonely years, overnight I was bigger and more widely known than Jesus Christ and Reddium became the international symbol of peace.

Now, it has been almost forty years since I gave Reddium, or should I say, sold Reddium at a very high price to the world. Initially I got my fame and distinction that I so yearned for and for my continuing research, I got more money than I could spend in two lifetimes. At this point, I honestly considered myself the true genius among geniuses. In fact saying that aloud and publicly wasn't considered anymore inaccurate than casually calling the sun bright. However, for all my accolades, my legacy is one of darkness.

I wish I could tell you that the peace followed, but it didn't. In fact, the creation of Reddium brought about a social storm that required a worldwide restructuring of powers. Wars were fought: many of them, but all in the more traditional ways of trenches and bayonets. While Reddium bathed the skies, the earth was bathed in the red blood of the warring young men.

Battles changed, but not like you would think. Armies reverted to basic weaponry because machine guns could not function properly and would instead jam up in the Reddium-saturated air. Jets and airplane engines would clog up, grounding the fighters. Air support became impossible because of the effectiveness of Reddium. In time, having a functioning air mask was more valuable to a soldier than water. And with technology crippled, the bloody casualties of men fighting feet to feet skyrocketed and battles returned to the fights of the First World War's the history books wrote about.

Many said I was the man who was singlehandedly responsible for destroying modern warfare and sending it back about one hundred and eighty years. It wasn't long before my discovery caused more bloodshed than good. Since it disrupted the concept of mutual destruction, it made the world braver and more aggressive. So instead of destroying war, I destroyed deterrence, and in a matter of decades I went from savior to the father of the world's bloodiest war.

As a child, I always believed that I would go down in history as the man who saved humanity, yet all these years later, here I sit in my rocking chair looking out a dirty, air-tight window at the red, hazy, war-torn world I alone have created. Daily, I ask myself, *how could it have come to this? How could humanity have taken such a gift and turned it into a curse?* I think about that a lot and sadly I think I know the answer. Because of me, People began to realize that the human race as a whole may be safer but their son, the one treading off to fight our enemies under the red skies, is not. Perhaps total annihilation was the only thing keeping our World Wars at three. Now that number is without meaning as the World Wars rage on without an end in sight. How I miss those days with all of humanity walking on the tightrope of existence. I have come to long for the time when the term "nuclear war" brought about fear in people's eyes, the days when political action went on for months if not years to avoid a confrontation and the super powers of the world would bark and growl but would never dare bite. I miss the days of blue skies and orange sunsets. And most of all, I miss my son: my one and only son, who would still be here if it wasn't for me and my foolish attempt at peace. I once thought that mankind wasn't ready for nuclear power, yet now I realize that the very weapon we all once feared was the only thing making us behave remotely human.

Tonight, I will dream of rose-red skies and I will wake up to them disappointed.

No Hunger for the Crows

A young, oriental boy sits cross-legged on the charred, war-torn ground and picks at the dried, dirty scabs that cover the bottoms of his shoeless feet. His lips, resembling dried-out meat, look scabby as well as his parched tongue lumbers across their crusted surface in a desperate attempt to wet them. Smoke fills the air of the small village as survivors walk past him casting brief shadows and a quick break from the scorching sun, the only help they give him. The sounds of moaning, screaming and crying surrounds the little boy as he effortlessly tunes out the songs of misery, rolls his neck, and leans back, giving the scabs on his feet a break. The leanness of his stretched-out body looks more like sun-baked bones than that of a normal, flesh-covered little boy as he takes in the surrounding misery with his emotionless eyes. The dead bodies that cover the grassless earth seem to be nothing more than annoying his view and the people walking by as they struggle to move around them, giving the lifeless bodies the same attention as twisted pieces of trash that scatter the ground. The young boy looks upon the cool early morning hell and decides to observe the agony rather than to join it. His eyes skip over the remains of life as he focuses on the living instead, even though some of those living barely hang by a thread. He sees a man holding his little girl's lifeless body. The father sits upright amongst the misery and embraces his own personal loss with all his heart, his own personal hell - the only thing powerful enough to distract him from all that surrounds him. The boy looks towards the man but fails to hand out even a single thought. The dead child looks just like nothing more than a doll in the arms of her agonizing parent. The boy grows bored with the father's bellyaching and turns his attention to an older man as he kneels down to feast on a small, maggoty bowl of rice. The passing people stop as they walk by to admire his snack. He gazes at them with the look of a demon, a warning that he would happily fight to the death for this rice because this rice is his life. He shoes away and lunges fast at all whose hands desperately reach for even a single grain, including the young children, begging and crying. Their pleas do nothing, as the old man's mercy has long since been starved away. As the first true thought of the morning, the boy thinks that he admires the old man; he admires his ability to survive and how he doesn't allow others pity or remorse to kill him. The young boy smiles knowing that dangerous creatures often come in small forms. The many parentless children circle the villages like packs of dogs carrying with them their own survival tools, big glassy eyes, hollow bellies and pity. They prey on a parent that has just lost a child who will gladly hand over every grain of rice they have, just to hug them and stroke their hair and close their eyes and pretend they were their own. And over time, the children bleed from them every drop of water and every crumb until their temporary parents are gone, drained and taken. Then they move on.

The young boy doesn't move in packs anymore. He's at that age where he's still a child, but his tears and cries no longer carry with them the same pitiful sounds that can make the starving hand over their lives. So instead, like a recent graduate, he is forced to survive through calculation and thought and by not making any mistakes. As he scans the camp for more thought-provoking entertainment, he comes across something new that piques his interest. It's a child whose life, at most, could have seen two or maybe three summers. Unlike the other children, this child doesn't cry or whimper for help, but instead just sits quietly, peacefully amongst the misery. The young boy observing has watched many children cry for days, leaning over their dead parents before moving on to find food and water, but this child looked like he hadn't moved in weeks, his face smoke-colored and his lips also baked dry.

Around him there are no bodies, no signs of a dead loved one. As the child sits up he wobbles back and forth, dehydration apparently just hours away from taking his life. The crows, dark-as-sin, large, carnivorous birds, stand several feet from the child hopping about in a pack of twenty or thirty. Their dark feathers are healthy, shiny as black oil and they position themselves with experience, ready to feast on the toddler the moment he falls to the ground. The fat and gluttonous crows wobble like penguins, still full from their last meal. Instead of being content, they circle the helpless child eager for another taste of fresh and the easy-to-chew human veal meat that cooks in the sun before their beady, soulless eyes. The young boy looks upon the child and for the first time in days, something stirs in him. Even though his pity for anything, including for the toddler, is absent; the fire inside him, his anger and his jealousy are still healthy. He feels his hatred for the fatted crows growing inside him. Those cowardly meat eaters just walk up on a prepared meal that life just provided for them with no effort. And for that they need nothing but patience. The young boy looks to his side and sees a bunch of crows feeding on the meat of another dying. The fresh blood covering the dried and caked blood on their beaks from their previous meals, soon to be just another layer showing evidence of their numerous feasts. One of the crows stops eating only to drag a piece of meat a few feet away: too full to consume it but too selfish to give it to anything else. The carnivorous bird then sees the others circling the child; it drops the piece meat and gathers with the others, waiting for different meat. The young boy grits his teeth with rage, watching all the happy, fat birds makes his grumbling stomach ache more as he grabs two bloody pieces of cloth and wraps them around his scabby feet. He stands up, grabs a small bag, and walks over to the child.

"Taeyang-ui naga!!!!" the young boy says to the child in his native Korean dialect, shooing the child to get out of the sun.

"Taeyang-ui naga!!" The young boy says again as the child instead just looks up at him, his eyes glassy and empty.

The young boy grabs his bag, opens it, and discreetly pulls out a canteen. This gets the child's attention as the boy opens the lid and pours a small bit of water into his dirty hand, which he has shaped like a tiny cup. He sips it as the child watches in envy, his tongue dragging across his crusted lips as the boy gulps. He reaches out, asking for some and the boy nods his head to get the child to follow him. The child crawls after him. They both cuddle up together in a dark, tented area, with a small campfire in the distance as their only light. The child continues to guzzle the water from the canteen. The young boy jerks it out of the child's hand. The child begins to cry, but the boy puts the lid back onto the canteen and puts it back into the bag. He pulls out a can of meat with a white label, covered in Korean writing. The child stops crying and looks at him with interest as the boy pulls a rusty knife and begins to cut the lid off. He has no idea what is on the inside. When the top opens, the smell of un-rotting meat fills the child's nose and, excited, he lunges for it.

"Jamkkan man-yo," the boy yells in a loud whisper, telling the child to wait.

The boy gets the lid off and exposes the food. He then scoops a handful out and gives it to the child, who hungrily takes it down. The boy takes a couple of big scoops down himself and then gives the rest to the child, who eats every last drop of food until the metal is polished to a shine. As they fall asleep, the little child crawls up next to the boy. The boy jerks back a little and looks at him strangely. The child just stares. The young boy leans back and allows the child to lie up close next to him.

The two boys chase each other through a small, busy village, down and out towards some newly planted wheat field. The older boy, who looks even older now, gives the child, who has now grown unrecognizable, his bag and takes his ball cap off his head, setting it on the child's. He then heads into the fields, grubbing for something to eat.

"Ani, geuleol sun eobs-eoyo!!!" the child pleads, saying they are not supposed to go there.

The boy looks back. "Dangsin-eun gyuchig-eul ttala jue-oss-eumyeonhajiman dangsin-i yag-eul deo meoggo," he says with a smile, explaining that he likes to follow the rules but he enjoys eating more.

The child watches the young boy go into a large vegetable field. The boy moves fast, in and out, searching for anything edible. He digs through the dirt like a groundhog and smiles widely as he strikes gold, pulling out two big, fat yams. He searches the trees for any ripe, unpicked vegetables on his way out but sees nothing. Everything else has been taken. He looks on at the child and waves the two large potatoes at him. The child smiles back at him, but as he starts walking out farther, an old farmer with leathered, sun-baked skin runs up towards the boys screaming.

"Geumanhae! umjig-i jima… umjig-i jima!!!" the farmer shouts telling him not to move. The boy, worrying of severe punishment, begins to run away as the farmer begs him to stop.

"Seodulleo yun! . . . seodulleo!!!" the child screams, telling his friend to move faster.

The boy runs and runs and then steps on something that makes him freeze. The ground clicks as he stops, looks down, and then looks up at the child and gasps. Then instantly, the claymore mine ignites, disintegrating the boy, his body now a red, cloudy mist. The child, wearing the oversized cap, screams in horror.

An old man sits up from his bed and gasps for air. His body is drenched in fright, and his chest rises and falls rapidly. He looks around searching for familiarity and sees his wife still wadded up in covers, sleeping soundly. He wipes the sweat from his brow and then lies back into his bathed sheets. He rolls over, kisses his wife, and crawls out of bed. He walks into a dark kitchen wearing a pair of pajama pants and opens a large, double-door refrigerator. As he opens it, the light illuminates the kitchen as he leans over and runs his fingers along the overstocked ice box. Every drawer and cabinet is jam-packed with meat, dairy, eggs, vegetables and fruit. He grabs a big bottle of water and guzzles it. He stops and leans against the marble-topped island, the fridge light reflecting off his still-sweaty body showing an old man taking a breath from his big gulp of water. He leans his head back as if the water was a drug. He brings the bottle up to his lips once more but then abruptly stops. He puts the cap on and then carefully puts it back in the fridge and closes it. He walks out and into a carless garage. An avid bird hunter, he has hundreds of stuffed and winged black creatures decorating his walls; however they are not displayed proudly but hatefully, showing an anger towards their nature.

He moves along a sidewall where three more refrigerators are lined up side-by-side. He opens each fridge, one-by-one, and inspects the full-to-capacity units with a careful eye. He then walks across to the other side of the garage where 2 massive commercial-deep freezers sit side-by-side. He opens the lid on one, brushing away some of the fog to increase his visibility, and feels the pounds and pounds of frozen meat that is once again collected to its limit. He shuts the freezers and walks over, dragging a ladder, under the large attic entrance above the center of the garage. He climbs up the ladder, reaches around, and pulls down an ancient green duffel bag. He sits down on the floor, opens it up, and dumps out the contents, including several containers of old, dented canned food, a beat-up, military canteen, along with an old wadded up baseball cap to hit the hard garage floor. He picks up one of the cans and looks at the old peeling sticker labeled in Korean and sighs. He then picks up the canteen and pulls the cap off, smelling the musky metallic interior. His hands begin to shake as he then picks up the duffel and holds it up to his nose, smelling its smells as well. He exhales loudly as his eyes saturate with tears. He takes another breath and starts to cry as he brings his hands up and buries his face in them. He sits on the floor and wails like a hurt child. He curls up in pain surrounded by his stockpiles of food and continues to smell his old duffel bag, allowing the memory to rape his senses and the agony to consume him. He bathes in his horror, fearing that he will someday forget something that in reality, he never could.

He brings the duffel bag from his face for a moment and tries to wipe the tears from his eyes, but misses a few as they roll into his mouth

With a quiet respect and grateful whisper, he says, "Naneun geudeul-i chugjeleul bomyeonseo gulm-eo kkamagwi jangso-es-eo, dangsin-ege pyeonghwaga nae chinguui yeong-won-eul gi-wonhabnida."

"I wish you an eternity of peace, my friend, in a heavenly place where the crows starve as they watch you feast."

* To Mr. Pius Yoon, a friend, teacher and Korean War survivor.

Rest in peace 1931-1991.

SUTURE

A Judgment's Sonnet

"Their worm does not die and the fire is not quenched."
Mark 9:46

The man clenches his bloody side and breathes heavily while staring at the woman. She gazes back at him with green eyes that are a blink-less still, now just fossils of what they once were. She is sitting down on the wet street, her head leaning back against the wall of the north building that makes up the narrow alleyway while her hand remains in the leather purse with the bullet hole out its side, widowing the bags contents and allowing the dim alley light to illuminate her dead hand, still clenched around a nickel-plated revolver. Blood pours from the stab wounds and a slash across her throat, giving the woman's blouse no proof that it was ever white. The man's face contorts as the fatal gunshot leaks his life's flow, rivering between his fingers and onto the concrete. He leans his head against the rusty dumpster that was chosen to camouflage his deed, yet now serves as a steel pillow that will deliver him away.

The man stands in the dark alley and leans his head against a door that reads "PAPA GIGI'S PIZZA" in painted black letters. He clenches his side, his breath remains erratic and his face flexed in pain. He breathes deeply and exhales heavily. He repeats this several times as his face unravels from agony's distortion, distracted by his breath that smokes up the cold air around him, a sight foreign to his home climate. He lifts his head and opens his eyes, savoring a brief painless moment, resting before another wave of misery. But this time, it doesn't come. The hand that clenches his wound begins to rub along the left side of his stomach, his fingertips searching to feel what can no longer be found. He stands up and looks around, seeing his breath become more and more visible. He wraps his arms around his body, bracing against what is now a bitter cold that penetrates his bones. As if hit by something unseen, he jerks up, releasing all his air in a throaty moan before falling to the ground and vomiting profusely, creating a lake of colored liquid that spills and splatters upon the alley's black asphalt. He vomits up what the living could never do until he finds himself surrounded by a puddle of what he has taken. As his vomiting subsides, he stands up and again braces against the cold, wrapping his bloody arms in a corpse's cross, trembling in a frigidness while he stands in his putrid ocean.

He knows she's looking at him before he looks up, the blonde, whose life has signaled the last of his sin. He looks at her with fear that makes his cold shake, stacking shivers on top of the shivers, rattling his lungs and making him inhale and exhale in short, desperate segments. In the midst of all his fear, he looks at the woman with a hate that poisons the air around him. He turns his back to her as he puts his bloody hands in his pockets and pulls out a crumbled pack of Camel lights. He pulls out the single last cigarette and puts the crooked smoke between his lips and lights it with a lighter that he pulls from the opposite pocket. He looks at her over his shoulder and then, with a nervous laugh, he looks down at the alley floor and shakes his head, tapping his black loafers, rippling the vomit pond that he still stands in.

"You laugh on the outside… But I know you tremble inside as well," the woman says.

"Maybe it's just the cold," he says with what he can muster.

"For you, there may be no more cold in sight after tonight," she laughs.

He looks at her again and then nods his head before dropping the butt of his cigarette and extinguishing it in the puddle of vomit. She gets up and walks to him, making the man put his head down stubbornly. He has the sensation of an intense pressure pushing against his chest, the weight of her divine omnipotence. She stares at him with her absent eyes, as white as milk, her head rocks back and forth, her arms hang to her sides completely dead of movement, and her posture is stiff and unnatural, as if the very supremeness is warping the feeble mortal shell in which it tries to reside.

"Can you not face your sin's own sight?" she says, tempting him to look up.

He brings his eyes up and locks them with the woman, whose neck spills with blood down her blouse. The man lets out a gasp and desperately looks back down to the ground. The woman brings her hands up to her leaking neck wound, holding them under the bloody faucet and rinsing them thoroughly in the dark red liquid.

She cups her hand with her blood and extends it to him.

"In case you've yet to quench your thirst for more, here you go David, just so that you can be sure."

As she says this she reaches out and grabs his bloody hand and smears on another layer. He begins to cry in response to her touch as he looks down at the pool of vomit and watches it as it heats up slowly, until he can feel the heat radiate through his shoes. The warmth thaws his cold body out, but only pleasures for a moment before the heat starts to sting his skin, making the bridge of his nose begin to drip with sweat like a faucet.

"What shall I do, David?"she says with a stern look.

He holds his head down, wincing in fear.

"What shall I do with an evil that rejects my light?!" she says.

She stares at him with her white eyes that chill his soul and carry with them the quiet patience of eternity waiting for an answer. She keeps moving her head around, causing her neck wound to continue to drip with the realism of something fatal.

"What shall I do?!" she says as she circles him.

What shall I do?" she repeats again like an echo.

He grits his teeth.

"Perhaps the mighty mute could answer when I call," the man says with a nervous stutter and muffled aggression, whose tones barely wrestle from his incoherent, inaudible weep.

The woman stops her head movements and watches curiously as the worldly and hardened man begins to take control of his fear.

"You could remain the innocent creator allowing this putrid destiny of yours to crumble," he says, building up the confidence to look in her eye.

To this, the man screams in pain and falls to the scorching, sickly asphalt that smokes and cooks beneath his kneeling knees. Under the skin of his forearm, blue worms swim, searching for an exit.

"David, they only feast in the darkness; they can't feast in the light," she says with a whisper as she looks down upon him.

"I don't even need to know you!" he says looking up and shaking.

"I gave you so many chances; now just leave me, and let me burn the way I always have, alone and by my own hand!" he says, waving the scarred scripture of his self-inflicted burns on his forearms towards her.

"Perhaps the worm's feast will drain your hate and you'll

call out my name for salvation's sake," she said.

"But will you answer this time? Unlike before? Or will you just stand silent and cast judgment on what is your very own? Just as you've always done," he said.

"David?"she says, shaking her head.

"Perhaps you should just carry this feast to your flames of sadness yourself," he cries.

She looks down upon him.

"Your fearlessness I gave you," she says with a persuasive tone.

"Yes, but you also gave me more," he screams as a singular worm bores from his arm.

"Take my hand to tame the feast," she says, kneeling down and extending her pale, blood-stained hand.

"Take my soul; it was always destined for your feast," he says with the quiet voice of a man broken.

The ground around them ignites into flames, cooking the sweat off his body

"Take my hand so the eternal flames will cease," she repeats.

"EXTINGUISH MY SICK SO THERE'LL BE NO DARK-NESS FOR THEM TO EAT!!" he screams.

"David, finish this life in the light."

"But my life belongs here, in the dark."

"Take my hand, David, and let your sin taste the light."

The old man wakes up in a bed tangled with sweat-bathed sheets that fight his escape and wrestle him in a mad panic. He walks across his prison cell to a sink and splashes cold water on his scruffy, aging face, staring at himself in the polished stainless steel mirror. He holds the old wound that scars his side and then sits on the toilet rocking back and forth, beginning to cry. The old convict grasps the small wooden cross that dangles around his neck and desperately searches the contours of his faith with his tender hands.

The old man lies on a stainless steel bed designed for death's transfer rather than living's comforts. A physician swabs a vein of his with a cotton ball of alcohol and inserts the needle with the expert accuracy of an experienced state-employed killer. An official stands beside a large clock and waits with cold, patient cruelty in the anticipation of a death a few more minutes away. The man looks over at the gallery of witnesses and sees a mother and father embrace each other as they prepare to watch their child's murderer pay the price for his worldly deed.

The murderer looks at a guard with the anticipation of his death and then he looks away, surprising himself as he begins to cry.

The minister grabs his hand. "David, do you remember your favorite verse for faith's sake?"

He nods his head as a single tear travels across his temple and into his ear.

"Let His words ease you into the light," the minister says, gripping him tightly with old hands with skin like onion paper.

David shakes his head.

"In Him we have redemption through his blood," the minister says with a calming tone.

David hesitates for a moment as he gazes into the holy man's deep blue eyes.

"Remember for faith's sake," the minister repeats.

"In Him... we have redemption through His blood," the minister says with a smile as David begins mouthing the words.

"If we confess our sins, He is faithful and just, and will forgive us of our sins and will purify us from all unrighteousness," David says with him.

"Their sins and lawless acts… I will remember no more," David says alone now as the minister nods with encouragement.

The suited official nods his head as the doctor casually empties a syringe, whose milky content travels into a tube that spirals into his vein.

"In Him we have redemption through His blood," he says, keeping his eyes fixed on the minister's.

"If we confess our sins," he says muffled as the glaze of death begins to coat his own blue eyes, "He is faithful and just," he says with the last of his strength.

"And will forgive us of all of our sins… and will purify us from all unrighteousness," the minister says, finishing the verse for him. The minister closes David's empty eyes.

David's blood-soaked body submerges into crystal-pure waters. He turns over and swims deeper into the clear ocean. With each stroke blood is washed off and left behind like a red cloud above him in the water.

Sweet Sealy

It all started with a girl named Veronica, but it didn't end with her. She sat three rows in front of me and one seat to the left in my high school geometry class. She had flawless snow-white skin, evil black hair, and a perfect pair of big, symmetrical breasts - the kind that made all the other girls in the room self-conscious. I would stare at her for so long that if I closed my eyes, she'd still be there, my cornea seared with her every curve. I became hypnotized to the point of drooling, just by the sight of her blood-red lips puckering up and surrounding that lucky pen cap. Her wet, pink tongue would dart back and forth, slowly and gently, stopping only occasionally to synch up those sinful, dick pillows and swallow the warm, gathering saliva.

Every August, when I started to dream of cooler weather, lusting for those cold winter mornings when she'd come in with her chilly nipples so sharp that they seemed as if they were about to puncture through her overpriced, and socially predictable Abercrombie sweater. She rarely wore skirts, but Thursdays were chapel worship days at our small Christian school and it was mandatory for all girls to wear them. This being the case, I would position myself in the back and over to the side so I could gaze at her smooth, creamy legs as she stood up to sing all the Jesus songs in her plaid, illegally short skirt. My eyes would start at her suckable toes and how they would flex as she periodically curled them to grip the soles of her leather sandals. Her silver toe ring, the one she wore on her right pinky toe, would sparkle in the bright chapel light that shone down upon us. It was those feet that caused me to develop a foot fetish that I still have to this day. From where I sat, my sight would then travel up her legs, to her thick, athletic calves - the meaty, sexy cheerleader calves that made me want to bite into them, but not too hard, just enough to leave a ring of teeth imprints. I'd follow the trail of enlightenment up to her painfully gorgeous hamstrings that went up her long legs, seemingly for miles, until the high curvature of her cock-aching ass would take my eyes off course and onto a butt that was so tight I swore it was made to be a bio-organic dick compressor, capable of squeezing every last drop out of my now embarrassingly swollen cock. I would have sold my soul in a New York minute if some dark lord could've guaranteed me five minutes inside that ass.

To me she was a goddess - a dream girl - but, like with most other guys, our relationship was only in my mind: a fantasy. Ironically, after four years of fantasizing about her every move and every breath, I got to the point where I didn't even like her. In fact, I began to hate her. She had never been very nice to me, or any guy for that matter, and she had become an expert at stuffing anybody's attempt to strike up a conversation with her. She became so concerned about being labeled a "ho" that she dedicated herself to being only a girl's girl and had developed a personal "swinging dick restraining order." What made matters worse is that a rumor quickly spread that she was a legitimate lesbian and that her lover was the same tanned skin, bubble-gum-chewing, hot blonde that she would huddle up with in Geometry. You'd think this would have been a good thing for me: two real life lesbians, the kind that looked like they had stepped right out of a penthouse pictorial, sitting three seats ahead of me: laughing, giggling and occasionally running their fingers through each other's hair, but it wasn't. I had to sit with my legs tightly crossed watching them whisper secrets in each others' ears while some crusty, old teacher preached the virtues of Pythagoras's Theorem.

After a while, I think my horniness started to cause serious psychological issues. I had this recurring fantasy that I would rob a bank, stack the money temptingly in a shiny silver briefcase, walk over to them at lunch, open it up and say, "Alright girls, here is half a million in cash. If both of you tongue each other's assholes for fifteen minutes in front of me and then take turns sitting on my dick , this is all yours."

Of course, I never robbed a bank and never got half a million dollars, so I had to relieve my sexual frustrations the traditional way: I would come home, set my heavy book bag down, lock my room, get totally naked, and begin to slowly masturbate, thinking about Veronica and her lover licking every last drop of moisture off each others' pussies. Sometimes I'd jack off in the shower, staying in there until I was a big prune. Sometimes I'd use lube, other times I'd just go dry. Some kids jacked off to dirty movies, but I didn't. I didn't need to. I always had my imagination and in my imagination, Veronica never said "No".

However, after a while, jacking off started to get old - really old. In an attempt to spice up my own personal "sex" life, I stole a couple of Hustlers and put them in between my Sealy mattress and the box spring. One night, I reached my hand in to pull out my smut and I couldn't help but notice how tight it felt. I pulled the two magazines out and then again placed my hand between the heavy mattress and box spring and began to think. After thinking about the specifics, I locked my room, dropped my pajama pants, and grabbed some Jergens lotion from my drawer, liberally lathering my excited and curious cock with so much that it dripped onto my light blue carpet. I then proceeded to squeeze my lubed dick between the two mattresses and began to slowly push my hips back and forth. It felt awkward at first - very different than my hand, but as soon as I started speeding up, my legs begin quivering from the uniquely exhilarating feeling. Within seconds, I blew my wad faster than I could remember. Traditional masturbation had become so unfulfilling that I had recently been falling asleep in the middle of it but this... this was different and, being the virgin that I was, it was as close to fucking as I had ever experienced. That night I slept hard, not even dreaming. I woke up and quickly dressed for school, looked over at my Sealy mattress, and smiled.

The next day, during class, Veronica was wearing a short, short skirt, (it was Thursday) and massaging the neck of her blond-haired lover. Normally this would have been another frustrating, dick-throbbing day, but not that day. That day I was headlong into Pythagoras's Theorem. A squared plus B squared equals C squared. Yeah, that's right. I was hanging onto every word that teacher said. I needed to get all my assignments done before I went home because I had a hot date - a date with a lover named Sealy.

I went home, locked my door, got naked, lubed up, and proceeded to fuck that mattress until my hip flexors burnt. There had always been something about jizzing across a bathroom floor or a bedspread that felt so juvenile to me, but I felt like a porn star when I would drive in balls-deep, arch my back, and come deep inside Sealy. As absurd as it sounds, Sealy made me feel like a *man*.

A couple of months into my bed humping, I noticed I was developing some burns on my penis. "Great." I thought to myself, "Just what I need, cauliflower dick before junior year." To remedy this, I taped two large layers of saran wrap on both mattresses. Then I would smear lotion on the super-slick, plastic surface and, just like how I imagined a wet, inviting pussy, I would have the most earth-shattering orgasms. It was so good that I couldn't look at my bed without getting a hard-on or getting flushed in the face.

For the first time in my young life, I was sexually satisfied. I looked better because I slept better. My grades were better because my mind wasn't so preoccupied with slipping my face under Veronica's perfect ass. And then the strangest thing happened: Veronica started talking. It happened when she noticed that I got a 100% on a big Math test. She smiled and said, "Good job," only to quickly frown when she received her flunking grade. Somehow, without knowing exactly what I said, I was able to convince her that I could help her and her grades. I was no longer nervous talking to girls. I felt entirely normal around them and she must have sensed it. Fucking Sealy had made me radiate some artificial sense of sexual experience.

We concocted a plan where she would copy off my exam without being detected and I would do her homework for her. The plan worked. It got her an A on the next big test, it got me a "Thank you, you're such a sweetie, love V." note and, much to my surprise, a real party invitation. Now this was a big thing. Not many guys were invited to her parties, so I knew that not only was this a big deal, but that there wouldn't be much in the form of competition.

So I marked the date on my calendar and Sealy and I trained hard for the big day. I conditioned myself to where I could thrust for twenty minutes before blowing my load even if it felt like I was holding back each one of my sperms, grasping them onto the sides of my urethra, clutching on to them for dear life. Every night and every morning, I did push-ups, crunches, and I bought a new bottle of Calvin Klein knockoff cologne. As the day approached, I got an outfit that matched my eyes and a pack of extra large, extra thick, spermicide-laced, no-fucking-way Trojans.

As I knocked on her big oak door, there was no doubt in my

mind that I would be leaving my virginity in that house that night. I just never imagined how easy it was going to be. When the heavy oak doors opened, I was greeted by a Veronica who could barely stand up. As we walked through the party, she hung on to me, slurring her speech and intoxicating me with her Captain Morgan breath and sweet cheek kisses as she apologized. She was wearing a sports bra under a loose pink halter top and a pair of white gym shorts so thin I could count her black pubic hairs. And, like I had expected, there were hardly any guys there. It was perfect. This was my night, I thought to myself as I held onto Veronica so she wouldn't fall or run into something.

Here is the part where I tell you that I didn't take advantage of her because that wasn't the type of kid I was. That I just went upstairs, tucked her in bed, and kissed her goodnight, hoping that she'd know I cared.

Nope that's not what happened - Different party, different person, different story.

After a couple more drinks, I was able to steer her into one of the many empty guest rooms of her parents' enormous house. I helped her up onto the big king-size bed, shut the door, and had her peel off every strip of clothing that she had on. I licked every square inch of satiny skin, every crevasse of her body, from her toes, up to her ass, like I had fantasized about doing so many times before. The way her skin broke out into goose bumps as I dragged my tongue up and down her inner thighs to the subtle little moves she made as I licked her pussy like a strawberry ice cream cone made my dick harder than granite.

Licking every inch of her, I was preparing myself for the best sex of my life, the first sex of my life. I was seventeen and so ready. Halfway into my "excellent" (her words) oral sex set, which from all her giggling was apparently tickling her more than satisfying her, she asked to give me a blowjob. "Why not?" I thought to myself. I had never had one before, but even with such little knowledge or experience, I was pretty sure that you weren't actually supposed to blow, which is exactly what she did. She held my throbbing cock in front of her puckered lips and blew on it, tilting it around as if she was trying to dry it from something wet. Maybe it was because she was so drunk or maybe it was because she just didn't know any better. Either way, it was terrible.

I hoped maybe sex with her would be better. I laid her down on the bed, and with her help, she spread her legs wide around me, while I put on my too-big condom and for the first time, I entered my first real vagina. Now don't get me wrong, it didn't feel bad... it just wasn't what I expected. For starters, her pussy didn't feel as wet as I thought pussies were supposed to be, or as wet as I had hoped it to be. I hadn't thought to bring any lube to the party because, at that time, I thought only old people needed that for sex. Worse still, the extra thick condoms felt like some judo master was choking the head of my penis, suffocating the blood, making it virtually numb to the touch. And worst of all, Veronica didn't make a sound. Not a peep. She just stared at me with her big, gleaming eyes. There was some heavy breathing, but that was about it. Sealy made more noise. In my fantasies, she had screamed in ecstasy, yelling and shaking: her body totally conquered under the pounding of my massive six inches. Honestly, even Sealy would at least squeak a little, when I pounded it.

And just when I thought it couldn't get any worse, it did. She threw up on me. I stopped, partially because of the vomit stench up my nose but also because I wanted to – fucking on a vomit-covered duvet was just too much for me to handle. Then she started to cry. So I helped her get dressed and I sat with her on the edge of that squishy bed for an hour, trying to comfort her. We ended the night politely hugging each other and silently parting ways.

Talking with her I learned a lot that night. Veronica, like me, was a virgin. She was never a lesbian of course; that was just a rumor she engineered to get the boys off her back.

Looking back on that night, it's interesting to think that there was a time in my life where I honestly would have committed cold-blooded murder to just be allowed to suck on her big toe, but after that night I never had even one more sexual fantasy of Veronica. No matter how much she flirted with me. No matter how cute she looked on short-skirt Thursdays or how much she played with the blunt end of her pen with her pink, wet tongue. All I saw was a little girl trying her best to pose as the woman that she wasn't yet. So, other than a shy smile on my part, I never really spoke to Veronica after that night again.

I had always known that humping a mattress wouldn't be the same as real sex, but what I didn't realize was that the real thing wouldn't feel as good as that Sealy. The whole time I was with that mattress, I was thinking of Veronica. The whole time I was with Veronica, all I could think about was my sweet Sealy. That stupid mattress not only felt better than the real thing, but it made more noise, it was wetter, and it never threw up Captain Morgan and partially digested Chimichangas in my face. Sealy never gave me any awkward moments or confused judgmental looks. And most importantly, Sealy was always willing, wet and ready when I came home from school. Veronica was a necessary experience on my journey of love, but I couldn't think of a better first love than Sealy.

I have since grown up and while, after reading this story, it may surprise many, I have parted ways with my beloved Sealy. After couple of romps with some women who really knew what they were doing, Sealy and I were forced to break up. I never could figure out how to get that stubborn mattress to finger my asshole while I fucked it.

After college, I got a job offer I just couldn't refuse: general manager of Mattress World, eighty thousand dollars a year plus health and dental, and not to mention a key to the largest mattress store in the state. That's 18,000 square feet of high-quality, super-dense spring and foam mattresses, and the most beautiful box springs that you've ever seen. We've got all the top name brands – Serta, Simmons, Tempur-Pedic - and a few kinky low-end numbers. A couple of times a month I lock the door, turn out the lights, and tell my wife I have to work late. Old habits die hard.

So, to all you out there who are so horny that holes in wooden fences are starting to have sex appeal, or for those of you who don't have enough space in your bedroom to hide a cheap blow-up doll, don't knock fucking your mattress until you try it. But be careful, you could end up liking it so much that real pussy, or real ass, can't live up to its own reputation and, like me, you just might fall head-over-heels for a queen-size pillow-top named Sealy.

God's Song

Grey's hand engulfs Young's: immune to the final poison, firm and fat, thick with broken calluses that prick sharp like thorns and a grip tight and crushing to the end. Licking his splitting crusted brim, it shines and shimmers with no soak coagulating on the surface of death, a thick creaming vanilla, as the layers bind his lips in strings of spit and he opens wide, whistling his air in and out with hardship.

"What's yer name son?" Grey says, his gaze glassy with ponder, leaking eyes that tear down a storied cheek and collect in crow's feet and pool like rain water in cracked asphalt.

"What's' yer name?" Grey repeats wearily, with a smile made for a stranger.

"It's Jimmy, Dad."

"Jimmy?" Grey says with an audible whisper, his face flexed with thought and eyes emptied of recognition, his hand shaking with subtle involuntary squeezes like a weak beating heart in Young's palm.

"Yer son," Young says with a proud smile and a straightened posture while rubbing his thumb across the rugged texture of a hand that fed, warmed and punished.

"My son's a lot younger," Grey says, wheezing in between words with a fluting hiss, trying to catch the air that is all around his lungs, but can't take in the big bites of life that he must.

"Small breaths Pa."

But like running fast against strong winds, Grey quickly exhales his catch, blowing out the access as if drowning in the air around him.

"You gonna be ok," Young says, tears filling his eyes, as he brushes Grey's silver bangs that stick to his furrowed soaked brow and dangle over his blue drugged sight.

"Git yu momma boy," Grey says, making Young's lips wiggle with the anticipation of an eminent paining mourn, the one that aches his insides, with a nauseous tickle that makes him re-taste and re-swallow his supper, all with just a ripple of the throat.

"Don't ya cry boy," Grey says, closing his eyes for a little rest as he slurs incoherences to the end.

"You's a… you's a good boy… you… You take care a momma," Grey says, pausing between words to tongue his dried lips a thick douse.

"Momma…don't…don't ya cut this boy none slack," Grey mumbles his eyes closed, talking to a past life, a ghost in his head that talks back to him. He shakes his head and dances his eyebrows while his lips squirm with dialogue of unspoken miming words that come out in a whisper, unknown, like a soft-spoken foreign language.

"What you sayin' Papa?" Young says with heavy breaths that stutter. Then the young man begins to cry like a bloody-kneed little boy.

Young extends his arms towards the old man and paws for comfort. The old man hears his son's unique song of sadness and opens his arms wide, inviting an embrace like he always has. Young enters the warm love and puts his head on Grey's chest and Grey squeezes his boy with his shaking maximum tight. Young's mouth lies gapping with hollowed eyes, like a high intoxicated by the papa smell of pomade, sun-heated leather and soap and safe with warmth like no other. The old man's gritty fingers stroke his cheek, scraping them red but with a hurt that heals and Young rubs his face against Grey's weathered grasp and then presses his hand on top of his, never wanting his touch to leave.

"Shh… shh," Grey says, running his calcified fingers through Young's thinning brown hair as the young man cries, drenching Grey's white issue hospital gown to a cloudy see-through.

"Yu… yu be ok boy… *shh… shh*. No sense cryin'… it's a long way from yu heart," Grey says, his eyes closed, speaking quietly like a prayer.

"We jus gonna get ya some ointment. Yu be as good as new."

Young calms his whimper to a quiet sniffle. As he rests on his father's chest, the final life beats, acting as a last lullaby that thumps with a sputtering rhythm against Young's ear, soothing him with the joyfully painful savor of one last time. His eyes tight, Young smells his father like never before, taking in and remembering, hard with ache, the pomade sun-heated leather and soapsuds, and safe.

"Yu gonna get better boy… yur tougher than an ol' saddle," Grey says with weak rustic cowboy flair, long and strung out, words like old spaghetti western script. . Young listens, like never before, remembering like never before the dark, gritty, short sentences. He breathes his father's remembrance once more, the pomade, sun-heated leather and soapsuds…he remembers papa's warmth, fire hot like a heating blanket even on the coldest nights…

"No more talk…." Grey's voice now sleeps forever.

Young immediately begins to play back his father's sound in his head, "Yu….you be ok boy," repeating the last memory containing his father's dark grit. "Yu's a good boy."

Young lies in his father's embrace and listens to the weakening chest flutter with nothing that could blood a whole man. He listens until his father's life's rhythm is no more.

Young stares at the cold shell of Grey, whose face is now of a stranger, too angular and empty to be Grey's, colored by ash and rigid, but still absent of soul's flex. Grey's arms stay close and lie against his ribs like skinny dead vines, his forearms pale and his hands and fingers curling into a tight grip that has already begun grasping onto the rig.

Young grabs hold of his father's hand that responds with a stiff secular chill of void. Again, Young feels the texture of his father's thick-scarred calluses and grit and braces against the stabbing pain of death's cold emptiness. Fighting the agony, he clenches his fist white-knuckled and beat ready as he begins fighting loss and it's nauseous whipping. He fights back, not with verse, but with rugged will and mental brawn. He looks down at his warmth, his love, and his shelter now turned compost. The room chills as a worldly cloud casts over him, blotting out the sun, the room darkening and casting shadows upon Grey's unsacred shell that no longer comforts, but scares Young with shivers that crawl through his body. Young looks at Grey with unconscious anger and fear as he watches his father morph into a dark laic demon of nothingness that frightens him to leave.

Young sits and stares at ice cubes, mating, shifting and slipping upon each other in a bath of Scotch. He sits on the edge with a thick blanket, shivering in the early sleeping hours and stares out at a dark sky that battles with the wanting light yet dim neutral glow of the heavens is the entire outcome for now. Young does not pray to what is not there. He is alone, with only a nihility that allows him only briefly to breathe a life of self-awaring matter. Nothing more exists for the purpose of witness. He shivers with a fright of abandonment and a loss, of warmth never to return a voice rugged, dark and soothing, with words that spoke the law, never to doubt breaths of black coffee, Marlboro and the mint gum that masked his vices poorly. He closes tight and listens and feels with all of his heart, but feels nothing but void and hears nothing but silence as he opens his eyes back to a godless chill and a godless world of mere coincidence and he is left only with maimed faith and frozen pain that will soon thaw when an emptied bottle clears his veins. He flexes his brawny farm boy frame and braces against the darkest of hours, ruled by an algid emptiness. He is tired of mourning and tired of crying and now just stares at the dark sky with red-faced, chapped cheeks, defeated and beaten by time and loss.

The sound of a child's shriek adrenalizes his blood: that thin, sleepy mope, chilled viscosity, circulating his veins to that of a liquid fire flushing him pink, popping his veins and standing him to attention. He shrugs his blanket off, hot to the touch, his heart pumping boiled antifreeze and acid, as his mind sheds the dull poisoned spirits and sharpens his senses to a razor. Breathing battle fumes, he rushes down the hall, cold as a cool breeze, as the child's screams startles the demons of quiet's loneliness, making the secular gloom melt under the rage of a soul that must be, that has to be. He opens the bedroom of a boy, blue and baby, powder heavy; the purpose of everything is found. Young embraces his child, who in turn embraces him back with a strong clutch and a tremble. Young holds the baby boy in arms turned to steel cables of protection while he sits and rocks him in an old creeker that sings its antique age with every rock.

"Shhhh…" Young says.

"Sharks!" the boy says with spongy eyes.

"Shhhh… jus' a dream boy."

The boy cuddles up deep in Young's grasp, and his body begins to melt in his father's warmth as Young wraps him tighter, the boy reaching out with his hands, touching his father's calloused palms with intriguing comfort, breathing in his father's scent of musk-covered Brut and scotch, the smell of safety that the boy knows well. And the boy listens to his father's calm but strong-sounding words that always whistle softly at the end, like a venomous snake that only whispers its respect.

Young holds his boy, who now sleeps, too deep for dreams to breathe, and his eyes tear up to a glimmer against the very bright, starry, night light. With Young's extremities cold from the cool air kiss, he cares not and he feels not, except for the state of his warm center, that he gives completely to the boy.

The rising sun creeps up from the horizon, ridding the darkness from its rule, as the cold's emptiness around him thaws to a fill and Young rejoices in the sunlight's warmth, the sounds of little lungs breathing heavily with rhythm that is Young's gift, and he hugs God's song for hours.

The Giver

We brought with us the reek of our people's rancor because our youth prevented us from having any of our own. They creased space and pushed us through the bright pain that brought me to my knees, and it was then that I felt the heat of a White Dwarf warm my nauseous heap as I leaned over and dry heaved on the seal of a ship portal while looking up with tired eyes that fed on starlight reflecting off a meteor belt at the farthest corners of the Milky Way. We all wiped the spew from our mouths and gripped our rifles tightly while looking down upon the pink Alien moon whose cities lit up just like ours. We came to kill and kill we did, and when we quenched our ruler's thirst for vengeance, we washed our hands, kept the memories, and sailed back home in a black sea of stars and emptiness. We craved blue skies and white clouds and fantasized never of women but always of food. I dreamed of flowers and fresh-cut grass and drinking water by the gallons while stroking my three strings until my fingertips bled droplets that danced and floated all around me. I remember her only like a dream, one with no real beginning and no clear end. I don't recall why I loved her, but I know that I did. I don't ever see her face, but her blue eyes are burned into the blackness of my closed sight like a colored scar. The way they swelled and rained when I left her behind haunts me to this day, just like the sounds of the micrometeorites bouncing off the ship's integrity used to, how the merciless cosmos would always seem to tease and test our sanity.

We aged like all deployed sailors aged and came back to a world whose time went on while ours slowed down. I watched many of my colleagues treat their great grand children like dying parents as the world we left was now gone and those of us lucky enough to come back got to bear witness to the most unusual of unions: the rise of the spiritual sciences. As free thought and logic sought out to prove the solidity of secularism, what it found instead was not to be expected. And when it happened, the world shuddered when our very souls could not only be proven, but they could be seen, they could be felt, and most of all, they could be given. What I feel deep down is that I did it more out of necessity than bravery: perhaps a way to exit a world that we all gave so much for but had forgotten us. When we came back, the people who tasted our kisses and cried tears for us, the people who loved us and cheered our sacrifice, they were all gone. And their kids were gone. We were now a forgotten story, just old text in history pages and were looked upon as something that belonged not breathing, eating or living, but instead, in a museum.

I remember it being cold, so cold my breath clouded my vision. That was the first time I saw him: a black child paled white with death lying on a bed of ice whose shell had been repaired carefully and ready to be filled. I gazed in to his hollowed eyes as we resided next to each other, bonded together by corded technology and things that an old-timer like me couldn't begin to comprehend.

When I awoke I cried and screamed from a pain so great it could only mean life and I breathed like coming up from out of the water and I was ice-cold to the touch with fatal scars that no living entity should wear. And as I looked through the many arms of grateful embraces while blinking my eyes heavily to fend

off the raining tears of a mother's and father's agony draining
from them, I saw a soldier whose body hung from cords in a dark
corner, his eyes open and empty. No praise was given to him, just
the remnants of a Giver who gave all to a dead child.

The real reason why Lieutenant Carl Rizz chose to give his
life to me will forever be a mystery coded in the blurry fragment
of a soul that we now share. Who he loved, who he lost, his pains
and his joys all live on and are given to me like jolts of electricity:
the persistent immortal spirit inside me that will forever feed the
thoughts of whoever it possesses. My name is Jamal Lester. I was
killed May 5, 2234 and was resurrected two days later. I am only
seventeen years old yet I have lived a lifetime. I have seen Mars
in spring and smelled the metallic artificial atmosphere of the
red storms as they whipped my hair back. I have shed blood under the brightness of a Jupiter-lit moon and have stared a frozen
gaze while sipping coffee on a ship that danced along the rings of
Saturn. I have loved and I have lost and I have heard the cries of
mercy and the sounds of the living pleading for life as I took it. I
am the essence of a sailor who left his life behind to fight, a war-
rior who brought the battle to something, an alien enemy that we
were told defined evil in every way, a dark species so wicked and
foreign it couldn't even begin to comprehend peace much less us,
but whose screams sounded so eerily human. Their agony's note
still torture my sleep.

This stranger not only gave me the gift of life but the
gift for giving it as well. You see a Giver is the chosen one who
holds within them death's death, yet even for the Giver, the price
of life cannot be exchanged without death itself. And like him,
I seek out a life worthy of remembrance. I look onto my future
with a hope and a deep desire to add a respectable layer upon
this ancient soul of mine. And when the time is right, I will do

what all Givers must do. I will one day look down on someone's cold end and empty upon their death until it is no more and I will give and give until life rises out of the deep nothingness and breathes a second coming.

And I will see it all through their eyes.

A Texas Rainbow

His long, thin appendages frame the window sill as he sits in its depth, stretched out with arms overhead, looking down on the mobile city lights that hustle about with an organized chaos. He closes his eyes and takes in the acoustic sounds of urbanism, playing the sirens that never end, before slowly opening his sight and picking at the dried acrylics that paint his porcelain skin. He fingers a faded rainbow bracelet wrapped loosely around his wrist, the pseudo-colors of expression give him little comfort these days and instead make him long for the real thing. He thinks of late March and spring storms and how the sirens only roared across his land when the frightful dark skies came with an aphotic rage of turmoil, revealing the invisible night clouds with a flickering bright glow, displaying their shivers, even under the sterile lights of an impotent shelter whose walls rattled with every shout the storm made. Yet he also remembered how the heavens would always seem to apologize afterwards with a warm kiss of prism light that soothed the soaked and frazzled lands.

His calm is interrupted by the loud banging and yelling coming from the hallway. He walks up and undoes the door latch, keeping the chain intact and looks across the hall, peeking out from inside his apartment at a large man pounding the opposite door with his fist in a clinched rage, breathing erratically and crying.

The light from his apartment illuminates the dark hallway,

getting the crazed man's attention as he turns and looks at the tall gangly kid with a bloodshot evil that makes him quickly shut the door and lock it. The man continues to bang.

He digs through a coat closet, slinging its content over his shoulder, littering the floor behind him before finally finding the dusty, small plastic box he was looking for. He sits down at a small letter desk that wobbles with the weight of the container and stares at the box in front of him. The light from under his door shows the room across the hall has opened, and the knocking sound now progresses into a turbulent argument. He watches his bolted barrier and looks as the basal light begins to quiver with shuffling feet, the argument across the hall getting physical. He stares at the door for a moment longer and then goes back to his plastic case, undoing the latches and opening it up, revealing a collection of broken-down, well-oiled gun parts. He begins to puzzle the components together with effortless ease, breaking away briefly to watch the door behind him. He proceeds to stack the dark, strange-looking fragments of metal and hard polymer until the shape of a pistol begins to form in his hand. He sets the final piece, a gun slide, on top, installing it in the locked position. He looks at his perfectly well-kept polymer .45 and grabs a loaded magazine, inserting it slowly into the gun handle. He finds the slide release with his thumb and gently presses down, making the firearm transform into deadly completion with just the sound of the right parts mating together. And as he grips his loaded weapon, he captures a peace that makes him feel a hundred pounds heavier.

He returns to bed, gazing at the blocky firearm lying on the magazine-covered nightstand and like a lullaby, just its presence puts him in a deep slumber that makes him long for what he once hated.

The old man chases a flock that runs from his pursuit with the elusive motive of knowing his purpose, but the man knows they know his purpose and moves not with athleticism but experience and patience and waits for the right moment. An aged hen, that has lost its fertile pass, runs right passed him to doom itself in a corner of sharp wire that shaves feathers loose as frolicking wings cloud the air with dirtied quill. The hen fights against the old man's grip around its thin neck with a stout jerk that carries with it a promise of quick mercy. With no hesitation, the old man swings the bird by its head and in lightning-fast motion beheads the farm fowl with just the flick of the wrist, sending the bird's body to the ground, still alive with movement. The young, tenacious farm boy picks up the beheaded fowl, grabbing it by its feet and hangs it on death-stained hooks, draping it upside down on the barbed wire fence, letting the body drain for the plucking. The youngest child, thinned to stabbing cheeks, pulls back and cries as he watches the leaking meat flow to a trickle and then drip off the blood-rusted barbs like water after a heavy spring rain. The young mother pushes him in the pen and he pushes back against her hands and digs in his heels. She pushes harder, de-rooting the boy until he finds himself next to the old man who is on his knees holding down a chicken that has fought to a still fatigue. He waves the child in, inviting him to join in on the easy slaughter.

The kid shakes his head and runs back towards his mother.

The old cowboy releases the bird, allowing it to flee in a cloud of dust as he looks at the young woman with a serious, cold stare.

The young mother locks eyes with the old cowboy and meekly nods, knowing what to do.

"Now you go long now... you do what papa wants," she says with a push before walking away. The youngest child looks back and watches his mother leave the pen as he stands trembling in the mud. He then turns and looks up at his father.

"Gettin' dark soon," the old man says, looking at the reddening sky, "best you start huntin'." The old man says with no mercy, making the older boy laugh. He looks at the older boy with a scolding frown. "If you've got nothin' ta do......." The older boy's confidence deflates as he walks away.

The old man looks at the thin boy and sighs, knowing that he has his work cut out for him.

The door slams open to the dark house lit only by the flickering light of a wood-burning stove. The youngest boy cries, his shirt covered in kill spatter and his hand drenched in a rich crimson coating. He holds on to the old man who leads him in the kitchen and to the sink. He puts the crying child's blood-soaked hands under the faucet and lets the water wash the redness away. The kid watches through soggy eyes as blood serpents swim in the fresh water that swirls around a pink-stained porcelain sink, devoured by a dark drain, as he blouses the white bar of soap thoroughly.

The night ends with the youngest child staring at a plate of fresh grilled chicken legs and rice sitting in front of him as he remains slumped over at the dinner table alone. He looks at his kill and gulps with no intention of eating it.

A man with a child's face, delicate and pretty, stands awkwardly tall and slumps with gangly arms that hang to his knees. He walks draped in comfort over style as a baggy white T-shirt lies on him like a flag caught sleeping on its pole during a windless day. Soon the bullying flatland breeze comes back hard from its pause and the man flexes his bone against nature's antagonisms while his shirt unravels around his boney beam, now whipping and popping in the calm-less breeze, like linen drying on a turbulent line. A crowd of knurled, sun-bleached cowboy hats, torn, dirty and weathered, match their wearers' faces, their skin dried to a darkened leather with deep wrinkles like scars that have blackened with the many dusted layers. One cowboy looks on with blue eyes that show youth trapped inside an ancient, thirsty face - a consequence of no choice. He darkens his lips, expelling his repulsive juiced vice, the cracked, desiccated ground soaking up the noxious flavor with a guzzling, grateful thanks.

Oddly stretched vertical with protruding elbow joints, the Gangle walks towards the starting line and like routine, undoes his leather belt buckle and pulls on it with a focused intensity, choking his neck-sized waist to a strangle, and continuing to pull with a veiny flex, passing the entire row of perfect machined holes before finally pushing the bronze pin through a self-made leather stab. He looks forward with a grimace, cracking his knuckles, while running his thumb across the four sacrilegious nails that grow beyond the borders of masculinity. His thin hands rest on his hips with limp, bent wrists giving off a feminine flair that makes the crowd of filthy hats stir with whispering opinions. He closes his eyes, rolls his neck, and breathes deeply before opening them back up and sliding his left hand slowly behind his back until his palm finds the hard polymer grip of a gun that he quickly wraps tightly with his long fingers. A man with a stopwatch blows his whistle, and in a flash a black large-caliber gun ejects explosively from an unseen holster behind him and immediately the Gangle fires round after round, moving laterally with surprising grace, right into the ejecting shells' trajectory, with them bouncing off his shoulder without notice, as he shoots five silhouetted targets with aimless speed, striking them all with flawless Mozambique patterns. The Gangle hides behind a mock-wood cover, breathing heavily but with control, as he pushes the magazine release and lets the empty clip fall out. He has another clip in before the falling magazine hits the ground and the crowd of baked and weathered men is silent with respect as the Gangle continues forward, firing rapidly at springing targets without flaw, without fright and with only the flinch of a well-timed trigger squeeze that always meets its target with an unbeatable precision that makes the stubborn, judgmental crowd clap with astounding witnesses of a gift that shouldn't be. The Gangle moves through the ever-thickening cloud of gun smoke, his position now only visible by the sound of popping gunfire and the sight of small fiery yellow muzzle blasts that move through the now barely ocular course. The crowd follows the sound and sight of only the gun, as its master plays his symphony of destruction camouflaged only by mayhem's exhaust.

The Gangle sits curled in a big city grocery store, his thighs touching his chest. He rests his shaking head on the frame of his pistol as nervous sweat coats his thin face with shine and his pointy chin drips like a leaky faucet. He looks at two dead, pooling bodies, still hot to the touch, their empty faces covered with the sweat meant to cool the living. One of the bodies, a woman's covered in blood, lies dead as her six-year-old daughter looks down on her, just standing amidst the storm of gunfire that makes the canned goods in the aisle explode their contents all around her, raining beans and cream corn. Her hand, shot to a stump, drips copiously as she paws her mother's leg, trying to wake her but only painting her mother's khakis red. The Gangle slides over and grabs the little girl, who does nothing to stop him, as he picks her up like a porcelain doll and runs for cover behind a frozen food aisle. He sits the little girl down on the ground, where she just looks forward, calm to a chill, as the Gangle pulls off her school dress and tears a piece of her private school blue and white flannel into a strip. He ties the strip around her arm, tying it as tight as he can. The girl screams, but the Gangle shows no mercy moving and working like a robot with training repetition guiding his thoughtless state. He ties off the stump of a hand, stopping the flow almost instantly and then drapes his hoodie over the girl, lying her down in an open meat chiller display.

The Gangle steers the filthy old diesel that chokes and smokes all along the rows of cattle troughs that go on forever. A young cowboy sits in the back of the pickup, his head covered in a confederate handkerchief, his perspiring arms brawny against the Texas sun and his damp skin catching every particle of dust the air has to offer, allowing the first couple of working hours to immediately lay their filthy layered tint upon him. He struggles to keep the automatic feeder steady as the truck moves along the troughs, slowly letting the feeder spray cow pellets into the steel feeding troughs without stopping.

Together they sit on the tailgate as the young cowboy swings his dirty boots back and forth, his cheeks packed full with food that he chews slowly, his face covered in mud and fatigue and his eyelids heavy and trying to shut. The Gangle peels an orange and throws the peelings down at a little cattle dog that hungrily eats them. The cowboy looks over at the Gangle and just stares at him with annoyance, shaking his head and pulling out a drenched Corona from a cooler of melted ice. He pops the cap off using the side of the paint-peeled tailgate and takes a swig, killing the bottle quickly, mumbling between sips.

The Gangle ignores his quiet ranting stares and focuses instead on tossing his orange peels into the dirt.

"You know," he says, pausing with a long build up while shaking his head, "You know… I'm glad… I'm glad you're fuckin' goin'," he says, scooping up a bit of dip with his dirty index finger and placing it in his cheek. "Bout damn time ya jus do 'er already. . . Been jus' sittin' on that damn pot for years bitchin' stead u shittin… tellin' me how much brighter the grass is on other side," he says, pitching the empty beer bottle over his head and landing it in the back of the pickup with practiced accuracy.

The Gangle says nothing, stripping his orange with more anger, as they then go back to their silence, but this time an unsettling one.

"You remember that time we got ya to pluck that coyote's eye, up there 'round Donner's place… Remember that?" he says breaking up the muteness with a topic that he knows will surely instigate.

The Gangle shakes his head.

"Yeah ya do… course ya do," he laughs and shakes his head, "Never seen anyone feel so bad over some dead red hound that's for sure… Yep… ya cried and cried and cried… Cried like ya jus' shot momma in the foot or something," he says with a smile. "But ya know what I remember most 'bout that day? It was tryin' ta figure out… how the hell… in all of God's creation could you done it."

The Gangle gulps a little, remembering the memory with ache.

"Shit… it was almost dusk… mile out with high wind… was jus' an impossible shot…" The young cowboy says, undoing his bootlaces. "Told me you got lucky… at the time I believed ya… But we both know luck had nothing ta do with er…did it?" he says, turning his head to spit his bleeding fix.

The cowboy pulls his boot off and dumps off the array of dirt and little pebbles out while rubbing his aching, rock-tumbled feet.

"You got any idea know how many fuckin' people in the world can do what you can do?" he says, goading his brother to respond.

The Gangle just keeps his head down.

"And what ya gonna do? ... Gonna go blow 'er all away."

The Gangle shakes his head, searching for the confidence to speak up.

"You got Colt, Browning, you name it... if they're lighten gunpowder they sure as hell got your number... And here they are... all waving ya in the sack jus beggin' for ya to hop in for a roll around... but that's not what my baby brother wanna do... is it? Hell no! He wants to just throw this golden ticket away... and go where people... eat tofu and shove sprouts up their ass so they can be more in touch with nature... Next thing ya know you'll be pullin' up visitin' us in some 4 bangin' ricer, asking me why I haven't been huggin' the cattle before slaughter."

The Gangle smiles and laughs, annoyed.

"It ain't fuckin' funny! And then you'll proceed to tell me that where you're from, they let you wear your goofy fuckin' rainbow bracelet and comb your little poodles till the wee hours of sunrise. Guess you ain't gonna be needin' this!" he says, launching his baby brother's rifle into the mud.

The Gangle looks down at his rifle on the wet tire-dug ground and looks up at him with hurt eyes. "Go fuck yourself," he says with a whisper.

"What wuz that?" his brother says with a threatening tone.

"Go... fuck... yourself... Dylan." The Gangle repeats.

Dylan smiles and shakes his head.

"Ya know... You didn't get all them ass whuppins growin' up cause yuz some fag... it's cause you always thought you were better... Better than everyone around ya... better than me... better than this place... Well I hate ta break it ta ya... You are this place..."

"No," the Gangle says defensively.

"You think jus 'cause god fucked up and gave my little sister a dick means you can git up and run away from all this."

"Um hmm."

He laughs. "Well then you go do that... You go run off to the bright lights... and paint pretty pictures for a livin'... you go chasin your dream! But I'll tell you one thing... It ain't gonna to work..."

The Gangle gazes at his big brother with eyes that begin to glass.

"God don't have no pacts with men when he's dealin' out hands. He didn't ask ya what flavor ya wanted before he gave it. He just gave it!"

The Gangle continues to stare at his brother, wounded and without words.

Dylan looks at him and grits his teeth, nodding his head and shooting another stream of black-as-oil chew juice from his mouth. He then lets out a big long sigh and looks down. He picks up his brother's rifle and wipes off the mud and hands it to him.

"How ya even know ya hate it here? Not once did I ever judge ya for how ya were... and papa iced his knuckles many a night in your honor. And, here ya are, all grown up... and you won't even eat a fuckin' steak."

He walks away as the Gangle tosses the last of his orange peel over the barbed fence.

The Gangle's gun barrel smokes as, breathing heavily, he looks down at the two dead gunmen, both dressed in black and sharing matching bullet wound patterns - two shots to the chest and one in the forehead. A puddle of blood forms under their bodies and soon grows into a pond that expands out through rivers of the grout of the store tiles. He walks over carefully with his gun still pointing on them as he tries hard to control his shaking hand. He kicks one of the gunman's rifles out of his dead grip, sliding it across the shell casing-littered floor and against the wall next to a young woman who huddles underneath a floral arrangement, wrapped up in the fetal position and crying in terror. She looks at him confused, not knowing that he is her savior.

"Shhh… shhh…" he says, dropping his draw and putting his finger over his mouth, leaning up against the wall of glass freezers. "It's ok…it's ok."

The sounds of police sirens and flashing lights engulf the front of the supermarket. He looks over and sees an older man looking back at him with a hollow gaze while draped over his shopping cart like a blanket, showering the basket's contents in his fatal rain.

"It's ok," he says back again at the woman.

"It's ok… shh… shh," he continues to repeat in a whisper, now saying it more to himself than anyone.

The Gangle saws his knife into the rare steak, expanding its bloody pool with each slice, making the dollop of mashed potatoes blush with color from the carnal soak. His mother, now aged grey, tries with all her heart to act normal in the presence of this unusual event as she watches discreetly from the corner of her eye her boy heartily shovel a helping of beef-soaked mashed potatoes in a mouth still packed with steak. His brother Dylan chooses a more noticeable option and just gawks at him in disbelief as he watches his brother wash it all down with a big glass of cold milk.

"There's more in the kitchen… now you get all you want," his mother says.

He shakes his head while patting his belly before wiping his mouth and standing to go.

As he does, he looks at his father's spot at the dining table, empty, and looks away with regret.

She grabs his hand.

"I'm glad you're back," she says, looking up at him with a love that only a mother could give.

"Me too," he says, kissing her grey head, "Thanks for dinner," he says, leaving.

The Gangle sits on the edge of the old pickup truck, accompanied only by the old cattle dog that looks at him with grateful thanks for each head stroke he receives. He watches as the sun sets on his father's legacy that still cools and relaxes from the long, hot summer day. The breeze gathers the smells of cooked grass and batters his hair back as he closes his eyes and takes in the sounds of locusts singing their chorus. Then he opens his eyes to the sight of several early fire flies hovering over the acres blinking their presence in the still orange backdrop. In the distance, he detects faint popping sounds that get his attention. He gets up and walks along the property line fence and watches as a young mother, kneeling down in the dusk, helping her little girl, no more than ten years of age, steady a .22 rifle and fire round after round at a paper target.

The Gangle sits slumped in a small, private waiting area with his head down. He looks at his wristwatch through yellow-tinted accuracy glasses that have his left eye completely covered and he breathes in deeply and exhales slowly, trying to calm his nerves. He reaches over next to him and brings the custom-made, long and blocky, .22 caliber competition pistol, a gift from his people, and brings it up close to his face, once again taking in the engraving that reads along the slide:

FOR THE PRIDE OF TEXAS - OUR RAINBOW

Underneath the wording, he stares at a small etched-in colored rainbow that sits above the trigger well and accompanies the lettering. He runs his fingers along the colors that make him smile with an emotional lip wiggle.

He pulls the slide back, chambering the weapon, and stands up in clothing draped in Benelli logos that run all up and down his sleeve, with a small section of his shirt reserved for the Olympic rings.

He holsters his weapon and pops his knuckles, looking forward with determination.

The sound of a loudspeaker voice echoes:

"Representación de los Estados Unidos de América en la pistola rápida 25 metros. Representing the United States of America in the twenty five meter rapid pistol."

They say his name and he walks down a hallway and out onto the concourse to meet his destiny.

The Good Man

Harold sits on the toilet reading a frayed Dodge Ram catalog, opening up the center tri-fold and lusting over the new leather interior like puberty on smut, his paper-white legs contrasting the red hairs that color his shins and thighs. He holds the brochure in his meaty, thick hands as his darkened, sun-baked forearms poke out of the light summer flannel folds that are rolled up to his elbows. He turns the catalog around, pushing up a pair of coke bottle glasses that magnify his eyes almost comically. The sound of a telephone rings thru the mobile home.

"CAN YOU GET THAT!!!?" Harold screams.

The phone continues to ring as his wife beats rugs outside with a yellow-handled house broom.

"HEY! . . . .Baby!!" he says, getting no response.

"Jesus Christ," he says, getting off the pot, throwing his magazine to the floor and reaching for the toilet paper.

He runs down the hall, zipping and buttoning up his worn blue jeans.

"Hello? . . . . Yeah... this is he..."

Harold walks outside, looking around confused before sitting down in a chair quietly.

His wife notices his odd behavior.

"Harold?"

He keeps his head down.

"Harold?" she says, but he remains slumped over in the ancient rocker, whose leather has dried out and cracked courtesy of the Oklahoma sun.

"God damn it, Harold!" she says, walking over to him, still holding a broom.

"Harold… for once I'd just love it if ya' would jus' pretend ya' can hear my voice," she says crossing the crusty, baked grass, wielding that broom like she wants to hit him with it.

Harold looks up with bloodshot eyes leaking down his cheeks, flooding the deep wrinkles on his face.

She looks at him in surprise as the rare tears roll down his chin and fall to the thirsty ground.

"Harold?"

"Leonard's dead."

"Oh … Jesus Christ our Savior," she says, squatting down to comfort her man, "What happened?"

"Damn ticker stopped tickin'." He says as he starts crying uncontrollably. The woman holds him tightly.

"As I walk through the valley of the shadow of death I will fear no evil for thou art with me," the group chants in unison, pushed by the intense, flat plain winds. Harold stands among the small group of mourners and hears the sounds of diesel trucks pulling up and parking on the gravel road fifty or so yards from the funeral.

"At this time I would like to welcome anyone to share anything special about this person," the minister says.

Harold looks around the small group that barely makes twelve. *Surely someone will come up and talk,* he thinks to himself. Everyone remains mute and still.

"Anyone?" the minister reiterates.

His wife nudges Harold, who looks at her with a scowl.

"Go… go!" she insists.

Harold walks up hesitantly as the winds scour his quaffed

part into a mangled ball of dark red, oily pomade coat, making him pull out a black comb from the inside of his ancient sports jacket in an attempt to pin his hair back.

"Yes! Terrific!" the young, frail minister says, guiding the big redheaded farmer behind the pedestal, dwarfing his man-of-god stature as he leads him.

"Hello, folks," Harold says to the small crowd as he pushes up his thick glasses and early sixties black frames.

"I wanna thank all ya'll for comin'. Leonard... he woulda appreciated it... that's for certain."

His wife smiles.

"Leonard, ya'll know... he was a special man. A very different man that didn't let a lot a people in close. He..." Harold pauses for a moment at a loss for words. "He... aww, hell! Leonard was an asshole," Harold says unabashedly, making the young minister palm his face while a small group of mourners all laugh.

"Yeah... see? Ya'll know it. Hell, that's why there's only about twelve of ya here today... because... well, not a whole lotta people liked Leonard... and ya know why? Because Leonard didn't like a whole lotta people. But, ya see, that's what made Leonard so damn special... he's... well... yeah, he's like that bitter black cup a coffee; you either gonna like it or ya gonna foo foo it up with a bunch a sugar n cream... make it something it's not. Leonard didn't change for nobody... and I know bein' his best friend and all, he sure didn't change for any of ya. And, in my eyes that's why I think all ya'll sittin' here today are special, not only to me but to Leonard as well... ya'll accepted who he was and, hell, some of ya might of even learned to like his cranky-ass, bitter ways."

The crowd laughs again as his wife dabs at her eyes with a tissue, catching the dark, mascara tears.

"I accepted Leonard for who he was and I put up with a lot

a his shit, believe me... excuse my colorful language," he says to the minister who nods in forgiveness.

"But I was rewarded by bein' blessed by the best friend, the most loyal friend, a man could have. I know for a fact if one of ya pulled out a gun and tried ta shoot me, if Leonard was alive he'd take that bullet for me. Of course, I sure hope none of ya brought a gun today cause I don't think Leonard's reflexes are up to par right now," he says with a smile, making the minister close his eyes and shake his head again. "I miss ya, Leonard. We'll meet again, friend," he says looking at the mahogany casket surrounded by flowers.

Harold walks with a gangly teenage farm boy who's dressed only nicely from the waist up with a respectable button-up shirt but torn and stained jeans while Harold's wife trails behind talking to friends.

"That old grump was as close to a father as I ever had," the boy says, his head down, "I'm still in shock, ya know... I find myself wishin' this was just a dream . . . ."

"It ain't no dream, son," Harold says, looking over and watching the hearse take Leonard's body away. As the black car drives off, it reveals several large men exiting their big diesel trucks and looking around.

". . . .It's a goddamn nightmare."

"You know those guys?" the boy asks.

"Yeah... them's Leonard's brothers."

"Leonard had brothers?"

"Now don't ya get all sentimental and go over and talk to them... they came here to fight over their big brother's scraps... and fight they will.

"An you gonna let 'em do it?"

"Gonna let em'? Son... you gotta lot to learn."

The young boy looks at the brothers with hate and they smile back with a devilish grin.

"Hey! ... Boy!" Harold repeats, trying to break the kid's hateful gaze.

"Look at me," he repeats.

"What?" the kid says, continuing his unthreatening stare down.

"Look at me, not them," he says, forcing his full attention by standing in front of him and jerking the boy's chin in his direction.

"Now I want ya to listen to me... you stay on your land no matter what... ya hear me? Now these boys... they'll nose around for a few days but then they'll be gone, that's for certain. Ya stay away from them cause they're trouble... and that's not me talkin'... that's Leonard."

"What they gonna do?"

"Ya know what they gonna do. They just gonna try an' sell everything and anything that's worth sellin'. You don't gotta like it... ya just gotta deal with it."

The boy sighs and attempts to start up another aggressive stare in the brothers' direction.

Harold puts his arm around the boy and walks him in the opposite direction, "If you get all froggy and go over there and start trouble, you'll get it with that group."

The young boy continues to look at Leonard's brothers with a look of disparity.

"Now, Leonard... he cared a lot for ya... so I'm putting myself in charge. Here's my number," he says, pulling out a wrinkly Pepboys Auto Parts receipt, flattening it out on his palm, and writing his number down with cheap black ink.

"Ya call me if there's any issues... I'm about thirty minutes away but I can get here in fifteen if I got to."

The boy nods.

"Now don't you even look in that there direction… Ya hear me?"

"Yeah."

"What's that?"

"Yes. Sir."

Harold's old diesel truck rattles worn metal down the dusty and bumpy road as he sings the chorus of a God-fearing song with his scratchy, out-of-tune voice.

"*Sail away to Jesus…*" He wails, his song infused with the cigarette smoke exiting his lungs and clouding up the cab.

He pulls up to the front of his old doublewide, a jet black Mercedes parked right in front.

He gets out, throws his tool belt over his shoulder, and puts a cigarette in his mouth. He tilts his cowboy hat up and stares at the freshly waxed luxury sedan, looking around, scratching his head.

"*Sail away ta Jesus,*" he says in a softer tone as the song plays out in his head.

"Hey, honey," his wife says. She is sitting at the dining table sharing coffee with a well dressed stranger whose permanent smile looks fake and well practiced.

"Hey, baby," Harold says walking over to the table.

"This here is Mr. Shoemaker," she says as the man stands up to extend his hand.

"You must be Mr. Colton," the man replies.

"Call me Harry."

"Ok, I will. Harry."

"So… I assume you come from Tulsa?"

"Yes… Yes, sir. I'm actually here in regards to a Leonard

Vint."

"Leonard been dead a few days now."

"Yes, sir, I know... I'm sorry about your loss. Leonard's death... it came as a terrible surprise to us all. You see, I've been Leonard's attorney for the last six years. I took over for my father, who handled his account for almost twenty."

"Leonard didn't trust many people."

"No, sir he didn't. In fact, I don't think he ever really liked me. He never was real keen about me taking my father's place."

"Is that why you and ya father weren't at the funeral?"

"My father passed away last Spring, so I hope his absence is excusable. As for me... well... I don't think Leonard would have wanted me there."

Harold laughs a little, "Well, I appreciate ya honesty and it does sounds like Leonard to a T."

"Perhaps Leonard saw that trait in me as well which is why, to my initial surprise, he kept me on as his attorney."

"Can I whip ya up something to eat? I got some cold apple pie," Harold's wife chimes in.

"No thanks, ma'am."

"Mr. Shoemaker, I apologize in advance for my ignorance, but I'm pretty sure Leonard never made out a will," Harold says, sitting down and scratching his head.

"No, Harry, you don't understand... I'm not a will and deed attorney. In fact, our firm specialized in criminal defense. What I do have is a key."

"A key?"

"Yes, it was a key Leonard gave my father, who passed it on to me. It was a key to a safety deposit box that had only three names on it: his, my father's and mine."

"Ok," Harold says, even more confused.

"I had instructions to immediately take all contents out of

his safety deposit box in the event of his death. The IRS tries to seal all safety deposits within 48 hours of death, so I had to act fast... but I got it," he says as he brings a briefcase up to the table, opens it, and pulls out a small eight-by-eight steel box.

Harold looks at the unsecured, double-latched box that can be opened without a key or combination.

"What's in it?"

"I don't know. Inside the safety deposit box was this metal box and a letter written to my father stating specific instructions on who this box should go to."

"And?" Harold says.

"And that person is you."

Harold's wife just smiles.

Harold just looks at the box, not knowing what to think.

"Well, I have to be going, Harry... it's been a pleasure," the man says standing up and shaking Harold's hand. "Mrs. Colton, thank you for the coffee. Once again... I'm sorry for your loss... I hope whatever's in there can help you all find some closure."

"Thank you, Mr. Shoemaker," Harold's wife says, still smiling.

Harold bends the blinds open and watches Mr. Shoemaker get into his Mercedes and drive off in a cloud of dust and then flips them back shut.

He turns to see his wife clasping her hands and looking at him.

Harold looks at the box that sits on the table.

"Aren't you gonna open it?"

He looks at her hard for a moment and then stares at the box on the table.

"I'm gonna take a shower. It's been a long day," Harold says as he walks past her, his sadness and confusion hanging on him.

Harold sits outside and swigs on a beer. He looks down at

the dull metal box in his lap. He takes a deep breath and watches the dimming orange ball sink into the flat, dry horizon and, with his last few moments of natural light, he undoes the two brass latches and opens the lid. Inside is a sealed envelope that reads "Harry" in big bright blue uppercase letters. He gulps a little and opens it up revealing a one-page, handwritten letter and a map.

A long extension cord powers a mechanic's light that is attached to the top of the open hood of Harold's ancient diesel. He holds a mini black light in his mouth and lies back on a little creeper under the car twisting and tightening and trying to fix what can't be fixed anymore.

"Harold?" his wife says standing outside, her nightgown whipping around in the summer night's breeze.

He rolls his creeper hard against the dry, uneven ground, scooting out from under his truck.

"Hey, baby," he says, getting up and throwing a wrench into his toolbox on the ground.

"It's late."

"I couldn't sleep."

"Why?"

"I just can't."

"Did ya open it?"

"Yep."

She looks at Harold, dying to know what was in it.

Harold laughs a little, "You know… I always knew Leonard was an asshole… I guess I didn' realize how big a one he really was."

"What was in it?"

He takes another swig of beer.

"A letter. I should jus' burn it."

"Lord! Harold, what'd it say!?"

"It's a Goddamn treasure map, okay?'"

She looks at him stunned, "A treasure map?"

"Map to the only fuckin' bank Leonard trusted, the ground."

"That's... great... isn't it?"

"Is it?"

"He didn't leave it for you, did he?'"

"Hell no, he didn't leave it for me! . . . Hell no, he didn't and I don't care... fuck... it's his money."

"You do care."

He sits down for a moment in a frayed lawn chair and flashes a frustrated smile. "I remember last year... I think it was... we were workin' up at the powerhouse. It'd been the third weekend in a row we been workin'. I get off work and there's Leonard in the parkin' lot... waitin' for me in his brand new diesel truck... the same one I wanted. Hell, it was same color. I know he did it jus' to piss me off. Hell, he needed that new truck like a damn snake needs thumbs."

"I remember that day. Ya were real upset," she says.

"Yeah..."

"What ya gonna do?'"

"I don't know... maybe nothing."

"Nothin'?"

"Yeah... maybe nothing. Is that so wrong! I mean, God damn it, maybe that's what he deserves, ya know? Leonard... he knew... He knew how tough things have been for us. He knew that... and now he wants me to sift through his goddamn fortune and make sure it goes to the right person."

"The right person?! Honey... Leonard had no friends... he had no family, no real family. All he had was you," his wife says in her husband's defense.

Harold looks at her and then gets up and kicks his truck, denting what's already dented.

His wife calmly sits down in his empty chair.

"He told ya, didn't he? He told ya who he wants to have it."

Harold nods casually.

"You gonna tell me who it is?"

"No. It's better I didn't."

"Yeah… You're right… you're probably right. Cause if it wasn't you… then your friend, *oh Lord, forgive me for speaking ill of the dead*, but your friend… he's goddamn fool."

Harold sighs while rubbing his face.

"Harold… I'm not gonna tell ya to do nothin'," she says as she walks up behind him and puts her hand on his shoulder.

"But maybe you need to consider that Leonard owes you some asshole tax."

"Asshole tax?"

"Yeah… and this is the first time you can do whatever you want. Leonard's not gonna get mad. He's gone," she says, walking back inside.

Harold stays outside staring at the bright moon.

The sound of the toilet flushes as Harold walks out of the bathroom holding a new truck catalog.

He walks in the kitchen and sees his wife as she sizzles bacon on the stove. He kisses her on the back of her neck.

"Mornin', baby."

"Mornin', honey, what'd time you get to bed?"

"Too late," he says while yawning and washing his hands in the sink.

"Sink out in the bathroom, again?"

"Yep… I'll get to her later."

"Oh… you got a message… from that young man. Leonard's neighbor… forgot his name."

"What about?" he says, his drowsy demeanor dissolving instantly.

"He wants ya to call him."

Harold grips the phone, letting it ring, "Come on… pick up, damn it… pick up," he says impatiently. "Hello? … They're what? … God damn it… ok… tell them I'm on my way… tell them I'll give two hundred dollars cash if the dogs are in one piece, alright? Just tell 'em I'm on my way."

"What?" Harold's wife says, worried.

"Damn vulture brothers of his… they're threatenin' to shoot Moses and Mary. The dogs aren't lettin' 'em in the barn," he says as he pulls out a shotgun and loads it to the brim with shot shells.

"Jesus Christ Our Lord! Don't you get in a damn firefight and get yourself killed for a couple of old cattle dogs! You hear me?"

"I love ya," he says, kissing her.

"Ya hear me, Harold?"

Harold drives fast down the country road, turning off through an open gate that takes him to Leonard's place. He drives right up the graveled driveway where a gangly older man stands over the stretched-out dying dog that whimpers in a pool of blood with eyes that beg to end what it never understood.

"Yer too late, boss," he says, smiling with his chew juice stained teeth as the big old farmer hops out of his truck.

"You shitheads! What'd I tell ya?" he says, walking up to the gangly man with a cowboy revolver holstered in the front part of his blue jeans.

"Hey, hey, old man… yer trespassin'," he says, putting his hand on Harold's chest.

Harold winds up and smacks the man across the face with a leveling left hook that comes from nowhere, knocking the man silly and dropping him onto the gravel.

Harold grabs the man's revolver from his pants and looks at the helpless and dying Moses, whose fur is wet with blood that drowns the canine's lungs, making the animals panting as useless as breathing underwater.

"This dog ain't dead," Harold says. "I'm so sorry boy... I tried," he says to Moses as he carries the dog over to the side under a shade tree where the grass still grows cushy thick. Harold points the cowboy .357 Magnum at Moses' head and ends his pain forever, splattering the dog's red memory all over his farmer flannel.

"That fuckin' mutt tried to bite us," the tall man says, now rolling over and spitting up blood and tooth shards.

"Where's the others?

"They were chasin' that other damn dog."

"Where?" Harold says as he opens his truck and pulls out his shotgun.

"In the barn I think. You ain't gonna kill me over a damn dog, are ya?"

"I ain't gonna kill ya boy, not over a dog, but you best pick up ya teeth and go back to where ever the hell you came from to be sure that I don't kill you for something else."

"Whoa! Yaahoo!!!! That was close!" a short, stocky redneck sporting a sweated-out John Deer ball cap screams to his brothers as he fires a 220 round in the stacks of hay in which a bleeding and already wounded Mary hides shaking.

Harold walks to the barn opening and sees the beat up young farmer boy sitting down, his pride more damaged than his face.

"You alright?"

The boy looks up at him. He's been crying.

"Get on, now."

The boy runs.

The brothers keep shooting mercilessly into the bales of hay, passing off the rifle with a toss and trading turns. Just as one catches, it Harold slams the butt of his shotgun in the redneck's face, flattening his nose and making it burst open like a pimple. One of the other boys spins to attack him, and Harold quickly kicks the man in the groin with his sharp, tipped cowboy boots.

Harold picks up the men's rifle and throws it over his shoulder using the camouflaged shoulder strap while pointing his shotgun at the other men.

He looks down at the boy reeling in pain from the groin kick and smiles.

"Don't worry, boy, that'll feel better once it quits hurtin'," he says with a chuckle and a wide grin.

"Hey! This here's our property. You don't got no right," the older brother says with confidence.

Harold walks over to the hay bale and peeks under and sees a severely wounded Mary lying down and shaking in shock from a blown-off back paw.

"Come here, baby, come here."

The dog lifts her head and looks from deep in the safety of the hay bale.

"It's ok, baby, it's ok."

The dog musters up all her strength and hobbles over, dragging the meat that was once her leg behind her with a limp.

The dog comes close and falls, but close enough for Harold to care for her. He pulls a pocket knife from his belt buckle and cuts the sleeve of his flannel off, quickly tying it around the leg stub of the dog while keeping a close eye on the gang of men that looks down on him at a complete loss of words.

"I'm gonna tell you something, boys, and I'm only gonna tell ya once. You might have right to this land and what's on it...

but that don't make it your home. This ain't your home, so you best take care of business and get out of dodge or I'll be back... and next time, you boys'll be outnumbered."

Harold's grey and white flannel is now drenched in canine blood as he carries the dog off to his truck.

"You're a disgrace to your brother," he says, turning around and giving them one last hard stare.

As he leaves, the men look at Harold with anger and nothing else while the one palms his still-bleeding nose.

The boy sits on Harold's truck and pops up when he sees him.

"Is she dead?" he asks, looking at the dog, whose eyes are shut.

"Almost."

"There a vet around here?"

"In town... about ten minutes, Here... take her," Harold says as he passes the dog onto the boy as he climbs into the passenger seat.

Harold goes over to Moses' body and takes off his torn flannel and rolls up the dead dog in it, laying it gently and respectfully in the back of his truck.

The young farmer boy pats the soft ground with a shovel, stopping and wiping his brow.

"Thanks for helpin' me bury 'em... Leonard would have appreciated it," Harold says.

"Ah, hell... ole Moses was over here more than he was at Leonard's. Hell, this was his home the way I see it."

Harold smiles and looks at the boy's shiny wet, black and blue face and the big lip splits that still bleeds on his shirt every time he wipes the sweat off his face and busts the scabby seals.

"You sure you don't need ta see a doctor?"

"Na . . . I've been roughed up worse."

Harold looks at him for a moment.

"What?" the boy says.

"Nothin'."

"What is it?"

Harold walks over to his truck and pulls out the metal box and throws it to him.

"What's this?"

"It's from Leonard... Open it."

He opens it and pulls out a map of his land.

"You know where that is?"

The boy looks at it and begins crying while nodding, "He left this for me?"

"He said you'd know where it was."

"It's where he's first taught me how ta shoot a rifle, under the oak trees."

"Well, good."

"What's there?"

"You know what's there."

The farmer boy nods his head.

"Good luck, son."

"What? You ain't comin' with me?"

"No, I ain't comin' with ya," he says while throwing the shovels in the back of his truck.

"Why?"

"'Cause I'm not. You gotta do this alone."

"Why?"

"Because it's time to grow up."

"Why now?"

"God damn it, son! Do I look like a rich man? Huh? Do I? You know, some days, boy, I feel the devil is just breathin' down my neck... and I just wish the good Lord for just once... just once throw me a damn bone and get him off my back."

"I'll give ya some, Harry."

"God damn it, that's not what I want, boy."

"Why not?"

"Cause that's not what Leonard would a wanted. Ya see, that's why he picked me... because he always saw me as the honest, good ol' boy he never was."

"That's a good thing."

"Well I'm god damn tired of it."

"Of bein' a good man? It's just who you are... Everybody knows that," he says with a smile

"Well, son, I've never held gold in my hand and been asked to hand it over."

"Harry... you're talkin' crazy."

"I just don't trust myself, son... I just don't. I'm not dangling somethin' I'll never have in my face. But, good luck to ya," he says, getting into his dented truck, "And you best wait till nightfall," he says through the driver's side window.

The young boy stands there shocked, holding the map, as Harold pulls off.

The farm boy slaps a loaded clip in the handle of an old 1911 .45 pulling the slide back and loading the chamber. He holsters it in the back of his skintight jeans and grabs a headlamp flashlight and tests it by clicking it on and off a few times before strapping it around his head. He grabs two big digging shovels, walks out of his garage and over to a property line fence, where he throws the shovels over before grabbing the top with both hands and hopping both legs over with youthful grace. He picks up the shovels and begins his long walk into the night.

The kid digs and digs under a big oak tree, exhausted and

anxious. Every now and again he drops the shovel and looks around paranoid while his hand grips the handle of a gun sticking out of the back of his pants. After looking around and seeing that it's clear, he cautiously picks the shovel back up and continues digging.

Halfway through the warm summer night, he sticks the shovel into the ground and wipes the sweat dripping from his face. Suddenly, he hears the distinct sound of a ground branch snapping. He draws his weapon and circles around, ready to fight to the death for what has been given to him.

"You gonna be here all night if ya keep stopping," a voice says behind the farm boy, who whirls around to see Harold standing right behind him with a flashlight and a shovel.

The boy holds the gun and tries to keep Harold fixed in his sight, but his hands shake. Harold just smiles back calmly and, with complete trust, the kid takes the gun off him and puts it to his side.

Harold walks up the front steps, kicks the mud off his boots, and walks in the house covered in dirt and sweat. He puts his shotgun in a coat closet and crashes on the couch while rubbing his face.

The shower floor darkens as the steamy hot water melts all the mud off him and he closes his eyes and lets the steady stream massage his aching back and cook his skin a bright red. His wife lies in bed awake and listens to him moving in the bathroom. As he walks in she closes her eyes to pretend to be asleep. He crawls in bed and kisses her on the cheek, and she turns around and strokes his hair. They fall asleep in each other's arms.

Harold sits on the toilet and flips through the worn Dodge Ram catalog, once again opening it up to a tri-fold, revealing a luxurious leather interior. He gazes at it with his traditional morning envy while running his tongue over his freshly brushed teeth. The sound of the toilet flushes as he scrubs his hands diligently, turning the orange soap suds into a bubbly white. He looks around for a towel to dry his hands and then sees his wife's pink robe draped over the shower curtain rod and runs his hands down the frayed ancient robe, fingering the numerous holes that run along the side. He looks down at his truck catalog and smiles, shaking his head. He wads the catalog up and tosses it in the wastebasket by the toilet.

He walks in the kitchen, where his wife sits at the dining table buttering up a piece of dry toast.

"Mornin'."

"Mornin'. I fixed ya some eggs," she says, pointing to the plate of two eggs sunny side up and some cube-cut melon.

He sits down and starts eating, looking down at his plate. She chews softly while not taking her eyes off him.

"Came in late last night?"

He nods his head.

She stares at him without saying a word. He looks up and sees her.

"You mad at me?"

She shakes her head.

"So… was it as hard as you thought it was gonna be?"

He looks at her and thinks for a moment, "No."

She smiles, "It wasn't hard at all… was it."

"No," he says with a mouthful of breakfast

She nods her head.

"We can stop by and get ya a new robe today if ya want." He says as he puts his attention back into his breakfast.

She looks at him, her eyes getting glassy. "You know… I was wrong what I said the other day."

"What was that?"

"Leonard, he wudn't no damn fool. He just saw in you what everyone else sees."

Harold sets his fork down and sighs. "I shoulda…"

"That's why that letter had your name on it," she says, interrupting his doubt, "Don't ya ever forget why he chose you, Harold… you're somethin' special… it's somethin' ya can't get in church… it can't be dug up from the ground and bought. It's somethin' yer born with, I guess… somethin' God-given. And you can't hide… people feel it."

She puts her hands on his old face and strokes his wrinkles as her tears begin to rain down her cheeks as he puts his hands over hers.

"I feel it, Honey… I've always felt it," she says with a prayer-like whisper.

Harold walks out of the main street veterinarian clinic as a bandaged up, three-legged cattle dog hobbles alongside him and he helps her get up in the passenger side of the truck cab.

"Ya know, Mary, babe, things are gonna take a while to adjus' but don't ya worry… believe it or not you ain't the first dog I've owned that had only three legs." Harold says, talking to the perky dog like she's a human as she hangs her head out the window biting the air.

"I once had this bull dog that loved to fight… hell, this little dog would pick a fight with any other damn dog in the neighborhood, no matter how big. And, hell, ol' Rufus never lost a fight… ever. That is… until he picked a fight with the tire on that movin' Ford. Yeah, that wudn't so bright… took his leg right off. Pretty gross if ya ask me. Anyway, yer in good hands."

As he cruises down a busy highway, he sees a young woman trying to fix a flat dangerously close to the speeding passersby.

She throws her tire tool off in the ditch in response to the carjack that no longer works as she hits the roof of her car in frustration.

Harold pulls up behind her and gets out, making the girl wipe her runny nose.

"You need some help, Miss," Harold says as he gets out of his noisy diesel and pulls a big jack and tire tool from the back of his truck.

"No… no," she says, starting to cry again.

"Hey… don't ya worry, little lady… we gonna get ya all fixed up. You from the city?"

"I was doing fine myself, thank you," she nods, her pretentious attitude exuding more than her distrust.

"Well… I don't know how they fix a flat where you're from but out here, a tire tool works better if ya hold onto it," he says with a smile.

"Whatever," she says with a look of harsh judgment while drying her face with the bottom of her blouse.

"Ya from the city?" he repeats.

"Yes… I am from *the* city."

"Yeah… I knew it," he says with a smile.

"And what are you supposed to be? Some good ol' boy from the sticks?" she quips back.

"Why… yeah. Yes ma'am, I am. Hell, I've even got a three-legged dog in a pickup truck."

She rolls her eyes, thinking it's a poor attempt for humor.

"You think I'm kiddin'… I ain't kiddin'," Harold says whistling, making the three-legged dog hobble out of the open driver's side door.

She looks at the dog hobbling over to Harold.

She begins laughing until finally it dissolves into a smile she cannot rid.

His Warmth

His body lies there alone. I'm so close; I can see my own reflection in the tiny, polished coffin. He looks as soulless as an empty wax statue. I am weakened by despair, yet it takes three stout men, grasping onto me with snow white knuckles, to keep me from scooping him up in my arms in a desperate attempt to meet his face with mine, to soak up his warmth one last time. But they know the truth and deep down, so do I. My little boy is gone. Underneath all the lifelike makeup is death - a once warm face now only a chilly room temperature.

I fall to ground in a nauseous heap. The painful feeling of my kneecaps slamming into the painted, concrete floor gives me a pleasant but momentary distraction from the agonizing feeling of my spirit being ripped from my body. As I vomit, I feel the warm hands of loved ones hold my head up, so I don't get it on my suit. The light pink, reddish remains of my obliterated and liquefied soul falls from my mouth and splatters onto the ground. My head spins as I look up from all fours and see a crucifix through waterlogged eyes. I summon all my strength and push up off the floor with my injured knees and lunge towards that large lower case "t" in an attempt to rip it off the wall.

"FUCK YOU!!!" I scream with a snarl that would tail-tuck a rabid dog.

I yell at that skinny man nailed to the cross. I yell at him so hard, I taste blood while fantasizing about burning that crucifix and that little man stuck on it until it's absolutely nothing but black ash.

"WHAT THE FUCK??!! YOU STUPID FUCK!!! HOW COULD YOU TAKE HIM FROM ME??!!" I scream, my voice shaky and cracking like a teenager.

As I stumble back to the ground, I feel my family attempt to lift my soggy body back up, but it's no use. There is nothing left of me: no recovering from this. I'm done. It's over. My hollowness is exposed through my voided, checked-out eyes. I'd wish for death, but it's not good enough. I long for that special dark place: that place where the constant pain of my burning flesh gives my mind fleeting moments of dementia, where I can forget about my loss. I dream of that unholy abyss far, far away from God, the mighty being who just stood by and watched my child die, like our lives were just for His entertainment: His little taste of must-see Friday night drama. The skin on my face burns as more tears run down that same path along my cheeks, dug out by redness and irritation.

My loved ones pull me with all their might back to my feet as I take a deep breath and allow myself to be dragged back over to say goodbye to my son. I close my eyes as I feel them position me over the body and then slowly I open them. There he is, as beautiful in death as he was in life, I think to myself as one of my heavy tears flickers from my eye and splashes onto his forehead. I grab his tiny hands, gently caressing and habitually trying to warm up his icy little digits, the ones that used to wrap around my thumb and squeeze so tightly it'd make me smile. I watch my tear run across his heavy powdered skin, bubbling up the artificial color of life, revealing a colder, darker truth. I bend over, my eyes now as wet as a waterfall, and I kiss my baby boy on his unresponsive lips, pressing my face against his pretend-pink cheek, begging for that familiar warmth of life while showering his body with my salty agony. I want to crawl in the coffin with him. I want to be buried alive. I want to choke. I want to suffocate and I want to die while latched on to my son. I look up and stare at the high-priced ceiling tiles, tears rolling down my raw face. I feel my father's hands, I smell my mother's scent, and I hear my brother's voice, yet it does nothing to comfort me. I arch my back and tilt my head up high, I crash down to earth once more, and I scream out loud, my misery reducing my voice to an inaudible, sniffling cry. My family desperately looks up to the sky for hope and peace while my mind takes me back home, under my bed and to a shiny silver .357 Magnum. I desperately dream about putting that four-inch barrel down my throat, violently gagging it down to where the cold metal hits my tonsils, and while everyone else prays to an empty Heaven, peace for me is but a trigger pull away.

I awake mummified in drenched bed sheets to the loud sound of a baby crying. I rip through my entanglement and rush down the narrow, short hallway, slipping and sliding on the hardwood floors with my feet like soaked sponges. I enter the nursery and rush over to the crib. I pick up my infant son and stroke his face. Immediately his searching hands discover my thumb, and he squeezes them with stout life. I press his face up against mine and, for the rest of the night, embrace his warmth.

One More Round

"Baby... I've got all day," the young, heavyset black woman says with a kind, firm voice to the old man, pushing ninety years of age, who stares down at his November-themed dinner with dread.

He gulps at the task at hand; his eyes scan the two pieces of dark turkey breast, turkey so dry it seems to suck the moisture from his eyes just by looking at it. He sighs and shakes his head at the thimble of brown gravy that hasn't been poured but squirted from a bottle in two long, thin lines.

The man looks over and watches the black woman pull out a Koontz novel as she fingers a dog-eared page and begins reading.

He picks up his fork and begins mashing the dollop of cranberry sauce that still retains the shape of the tin can it came from. He catches the woman's eyes non-discreetly peeking over her book for just a moment, but then diving back.

He forks off a piece of the firm cranberry jelly and puts it in his mouth. As he chews, he can taste a hint of tin. To get the sweet taste from his mouth, he forks off a piece of turkey and puts it on his tongue. The salty, dry meat makes him reach for his beverage in a mad panic as if he's choking, and he quickly drowns the bite with a gulp of water. The salty aftermath is so bad that he considers another bite of tin sauce to counteract his bite of salted turkey.

"Just eat ya' damn food."

"It's a salt lick," he says with a mind as sharp as a fifty-year-old but a body of a starving prisoner.

"It ain't that bad, John."

"Here… taste," he says, reaching a bite up to her lips.

"I'm on a diet," she says, shoving the fork from her face.

"A diet?" he repeats with a smile.

"Yeah John… a diet," she says defensively.

"Y'ain't ever gonna be a skinny girl."

"And why is that?" she says.

"Same reason a shark'll never be a minnow. You see, you colored folk…"

"Colored folk?"

"I noticed y'all seem ta have hearty appetites… and… you know what? That's alright. That's the way God made ya. And if that's the way god made ya… then that's ok in my book."

"Uh hum."

"Don't be fighting mother-nature, darlin'… you're wrestling with the wind. Big girls like you got big appetites. That's the way it is. That's the way it's always been."

She glares at him, hateful fumes steaming from her eyes.

"Personally I'm not a fan of gluttonous behavior even if it's natural for some… but the good Lord says judge not or thou shall be judged," he says, scooting his plate to her.

"What on Earth are you doin?" the woman says, watching him push the plate under her nose.

"Listen, I'm just gonna look the other way… and, well… if my plate gets cleaned… then, I guess I was real hungry today."

"John."

"You look hungry, Nike," he pronounces like the shoe.

"It's Nikkia. "

"Nicky?"

"Mr. Crowl… Eat! Now!" she says, putting the fork in his

hand and pushing the plate back under his frown.

The old man looks at what's left of his plate and gulps as if he were about to run ten miles.

"It's real simple, Dad... there's forward... there's backwards... there's left... and there's right..." the young man says as he maneuvers the wheelchair around, demonstrating its operation.

"You think you got it?" he says to the old man, who lies in the bed with sleepy eyes and a steady stream of oxygen running up clear lines into his nostrils.

The old man looks on at his son with grumpy annoyance and sighs.

"What'dya mean, '*do I got it?*' Of course, I got it," he says with a sigh as he turns and looks at his son's wife, a beautiful brunette who is holding onto a sleeping newborn.

"Dad... I was just..."

"Does he talk ta you like this?" he says interrupting.

"Sometimes," she says with a smile.

"You know... I told him, '*Jimmy, I'd sure love to have some grandkids someday*'... and what does he do? He waits till I'm ninety-one. Ninety one!"

"It's called waiting for true love, Dad."

The old man rolls his eyes and groans.

"I'm gonna be dead before my granddaughter sprouts her first tooth."

"Oh come on... you're gonna live to be a hundred. Now try out your new wheels," he says with a smile as he helps the old man sit up.

"I got it, I got it, I got it..." he says, pawing his sons arms off as he strenuously sets himself up.

"Ok… now remember your controls," the young man says as the old man starts yanking on the joystick and it does nothing.

"Let me guess… made in China."

"Ok, stop for a minute…"

"Hope ya didn't pay over a nickel for this piece of crap," he says, still shifting.

"Stop for a minute… what are we forgetting?"

He keeps jerking the controller.

"Dad! Stop for a minute!"

He gives him a blank look.

"The 'on' button, dad," the son says, pushing it and lighting up the control panel.

"Hmm," the old man says, looking down.

"Now, before you run…"

Immediately the old man interrupts his son again and hits it in reverse, accidently running the back wheel over his son's toes.

"OW!… FUCK!!!! " he says hobbling all over the place. "Fuck, fuck, fuck, fuck… ow!"

"Oh… Jesus, son… I'm sorry. Are you ok?" he says with a little chuckle.

"It's not funny, Dad."

"I'm sorry, son, but you're wrong… It was funny," he says, making his son's wife laugh.

"Don't encourage him Babe," the son says as he rubs his big toe.

"I'm sorry, it *was* funny!" his wife confirms.

Jimmy just massages his toes with a wince.

The old man hits forward and rams the wheelchair into the side of the bed. "Woops…"

The wife just keeps laughing as she watches her father-in-law try to maneuver the electric chair.

"Piece of shit!" the old man yells as he continuously knocks things over his room, driving the electric scooter as if it were a bumper car at the fair. His son's wife is now laughing so hard she cannot breathe, while the young man sits down and continues to rub his feet.

The old man sits in his chair and watches the rain smack against the dirty window and rinse off the thick layer of dust that has hampered his view all season. The window cries in streams as the dirty sadness pools on the window sill, and in the distance the cloudy bay melts away, revealing a clear transparency that makes him doubt his own cataracts. He stares at a young maple swaying modestly from side to side and watches the tree as it valiantly battles it out with the stout fall storm with youthful strength and flexibility. Little flashes of bright light supersede the crashing thunder. John sits completely still, reaction-less to the violent storm that bows and flexes the windows as an angry heaven strikes the ground with a white fire demanding respect. The old man does not give the turmoil in the sky even a blink. He sits and lets the bright, glowing clouds illuminate his corpsed eyes like a warm death whose heart beats but whose spirit sleeps.

John sits across the table with an old woman whose hand shakes off the piece of blueberry pie from her fork. John walks over to her side of the table and sits close to her left.

"Let me," he says as he cuts a new piece of butter-crusted blueberry cobbler and feeds it to her. She smiles at him. His hand gently pins hers as they sit in the commons area together and watch Wheel of Fortune.

"GREENICH VILLAGE," she says proudly moments before the host repeats her.

John smiles at her smile.

All of a sudden the TV switches channels to the weather.

"Hey!" John says turning around and finding another man manning the TV remote.

"It's ok… your show is almost over."

"It's not ok," he says as he walks up to the television and changes it back manually.

Before he can get back to his seat, the channel switches back.

"Ok…" John says, walking over to the man.

"Can you please turn it back? We were watching that show."

"Your sweetheart ova' there? She been watchin' two hours of game shows," he says with a thick, Bostonian accent.

"So?"

"So it's time ta share."

John walks back over to the TV and turns back to the channel with the game show, and the man quickly switches it back with the remote. John switches it back to his channel again, and the man switches it back with a laugh.

John walks over.

"Give," he says, signaling with his hand that he wants the remote.

"No," the man says. A couple of his friends laugh with him.

"Now."

"Or what?"

John punches him square in the nose.

"Mr. Crowl, do you know where the remote is?" A police officer is talking to John, who is sitting in a chair, his head down and his right hand wrapped in ice.

John shrugs.

"Mr. Crowl… that remote is not your property. If you have it, it means you have in your possession stolen property," the police officer repeats, frustrated.

"I don't know where the damn remote is."

"Do you know what assault charges are?"

John laughs.

The police officer looks at him, irritated.

"Of course you do. You haven't changed a bit... have you, Lieutenant?"

The old man looks up at him, surprised.

"You worked with my father, Stacker, Matt Stacker," the officer says.

The old man just looks at him.

"Remember?"

"It was a long time ago."

"But you *do* remember?"

The old man pauses for a moment. He nods his head. The cop looks at him expecting a response.

"He was an asshole."

The police officer bursts into laughter.

"Yeah... you're right, he was. But in his defense, he felt the same about you."

"That's because your mother never got over me."

The cop looks at him, his smile dissolving.

"How is sweet Rebecca doing these days?"

"She's dead."

John shrugs.

"Mr. Crowl... if you hit anyone again, I'm gonna take ya in."

John smirks.

"Go ahead... think I'm kidding. I don't care if it's your birthday and you're turning a hundred," he says as he then leans in and whispers into his ear, "I'll lock your cranky ass up with two big ol' horny niggers that'll just love your soft, old squishy prostate," he says with a smile.

"The apple sure doesn't fall far from a tree, huh?" the old

man says.

"Just telling ya how it is, old man."

John puts his head back down as the officer walks away.

John sits next to the older woman, whose deathbed has re-mained warm for days now. She looks at him and flashes a little smile while her medications keep her eyes sleepy and without pain.

"Am I dying?" She asks.

He looks down at her and nods.

"How much longer."

"I don't know."

"Wesley... I'm scared."

"Don't be," John says as he embraces her.

"Ok," she says.

John sleeps on the couch next to the old lady. He is awak-ened by the sound of the door opening and a woman and her husband walking in.

"Oh!" she says, startled by John as she comes around the corner.

"Oh, god... you scared me," she says, grabbing her chest.

"I'm sorry."

The woman looks at her mother and leans over to kiss her while John just stands there.

"And you are?" the husband says.

"I'm John," he says as he looks at the woman stroking her mother's hair. "She didn't... she didn't want to be left alone."

"Of course not...You sound like... like a good friend."

"Not as good as she deserved."

They both share an awkward silence

"Well, John we sure appreciate ya" he says extending out his hand. "I think we got it from here."

John looks at the man's hand and then nods his head in understanding.

"We've got a lot of family comin' in… I hope you understand."

"Sure," he says.

The daughter looks up at John, tears rolling from her eyes.

"May I?" John asks the daughter for a final goodbye.

She nods.

John looks down at the old woman and strokes her face and gazes at her skin-coated eyes. He leans down and gives her a deep, passionate kiss on the lips that lingers. He kisses her not like a friend, but a lover.

The daughter looks on in disbelief.

John finally breaks away his kiss, looks down at her, and leaves. The couple stares - stunned at the man as he walks out of the room. He shuts the door and for a moment stares at it closed. He leans his head against the door and brings his shaking hand back up to the doorknob. His eyes are glassy with pain as he clenches his hand tightly, resisting the urge to open up the door again. He takes several deep breaths, wipes his tears, and walks away.

"We gather here today to remember Ginger Ann D'Sol," the black-suited minister says in an outdoor graveside ceremony on a bright but windy day.

"Ginger was born in Fayetteville, Arkansas on October 31, 1919, where she lived until graduating with honors from New Cherish Catholic high school in 1934," the minister says, fighting to keep his speech notes intact as the wind flips the paper's corners up, begging to abduct the yellow notes.

John sits in the chair farthest back. With his son as he looks around at the few hundred plus attendees.

"The youngest of eight siblings, she was the only one to attend a university where she became a schoolteacher and met her husband, Wesley D'Sol," the minister says as his tie flips and turns across his face in response to the chilly gusts.

"They were married in 1937 and were together for 56 years until her husband's passing. An avid humanitarian and philanthropist, Ginger was very active with her church's community outreach projects and even served as outreach director for four years after her retirement," the minister says with sorrowful smile to the front row of loved ones who loved her most and who show it with sobs and gentle dabs to their eyes with wadded Kleenex.

"Ginger's life will always be remembered for her kind and selfless actions, as well as her optimistic attitude. Ginger is survived by her four sons, John, Jacob, Jesse, and Bill as well as nine grandchildren and four great grandchildren."

John stands close to the now desolate graveside and looks at his aged reflection in the waxed surface of the closed casket, surrounded by spring-colored flowers. His son remains in the background with a sweater draped over his shoulders as he gives his grieving father some privacy. John looks at the picture of Ginger. It is a young picture, not a picture of the Ginger he knew. He reaches into his out-of-fashion sports coat and pulls out the television remote. He rests it on top of the firm, fresh-cut flowers that don't even budge under its weight. He walks away and towards his grown boy, who consoles him with a draped arm as they walk back to their car.

"You sure you don't want anything to eat?" his son says, pulling up to the assisted living community.

The old man shakes his head.

"You haven't eaten anything today, have you?"

The old man puts his head, down rubbing his face.

His son sighs a bit, annoyed by his father's nonexistent appetite, but he keeps it to himself.

"I'm so sorry about your friend, Dad," His son says.

The old man begins to nod his head.

"She was…" he says, choking up and cutting off his sentence as he bites his quivering lip, pausing for a moment to regain his bearings. "She was my woman," he says as he looks at his son with waterlogged eyes.

His son just looks at his father, surprised.

\---

The big black woman tries to spoon-feed John, who just sits in his chair and stares away. He opens his mouth half heartedly making the grits leak out of the corner of his mouth.

"Oh I see how it is… you gonna make me work for my money today… huh?" she says with a smile as she gently wipes his mouth. Oxygen cords wrap around his face and into his nose as he sits in his wheelchair and she brings a cup of water to his mouth.

He looks at the nurse and smiles.

" … Thank you…"

"You're welcome baby"

"Are you my angel?"

"Angels don't wear makeup."

"I'm tired," he says.

"I know."

"I won't make you eat anymore… but I'm gonna fetch you some more water… and you're gonna drink it… all of it… or I'm gonna have ta stick you… Ok?"

He looks away.

"Hey…" she says, grabbing his chin and pulling it in her direction.

"Ok."

He nods and watches her walk away.

He gazes at the fireplace, across the dining room and into the commons area where the old people play their games and watch their television. He focuses in on the flames of the large wood-burning stove and watches as the fire flickers against the blackened glass and begins to drift him to sleep. His eyelids feel as heavy as anvils as they close.

"And this is the commons area." The sound of Meadowview South's new account manager's sales pitch radiates through the room as he talks to a young couple escorting an older woman with porcelain sun-starved skin and long grey hair that looks strong, thick and heavy, like millions of tiny strands of steel. The old man's sleepy eyes open a bit as he watches her walk around with a beautiful smile, displaying teeth as white as her flawless skin. He watches carefully as she greets some of the tenants as the young couple, apparently impressed by the facility tour, shakes the manager's hands.

"I have some papers for you to sign," the manager says as he leads the couple to his office.

John takes notice.

John sits in a dark room, gazing at the television but not watching it, the whistling sounds of his oxygen tubes pushing air into his nostrils. His eyes window a soul paused in time, as they remain fixed open and glassy from the blink-less stares of exit, his lips crusted with dehydration, cracked like droughted ground.

A young man in a military uniform smiles at the beautiful young brunette woman draped in wedding white as he places a modest silver band on her finger. With encouragement from the minister, they kiss with passionate class.

John's eyes blink more than they have in weeks as his

tongue waters his chapped lips. He sits up from his slump and rolls his neck, making it sing with pops and cracks. He pulls the breathing tubes from his nose and immediately starts to fall short of breath. His shallow, weak inhalations do nothing to satisfy his old, spoiled, and lazy lungs. He clenches his fist and grits his teeth as he forces his chest to rise, forcing his stiff lungs to expand. He continues this painful process until his face is red and a thin coat of sweat begins to bead on his old, spotty forehead. Soon his breathing becomes smoother, his clenched fists relaxing. He slides his feet out of the footrest peddles and places them on the ground in front of him. With all his power, and with quivering arms, he pulls himself out of the chair and stands halfway up, his legs wobbling from gravity's strain. He then falls back, crumbling into his wheelchair in an exhausted state. Wheezing and gasping for air, he closes his eyes and again takes in three or four deep breaths and pulls himself up to standing. He stands up on his weak, shaky legs and then sits back down before resting and repeating it all over again.

The big black woman looks on in shock as John devours his dry meatloaf, shoveling it in like a growing teenager. With a mouthful of oatmeal grain and beef, he drinks the final sip of white milk before wiping his mouth with his napkin and rolling away.

"Thank you darling," he says to the surprised woman, who gives him no response as he backs up his chair and rolls away.

In his room with a towel draped around his neck, he stands up from his wheelchair and then back down again, finishing a set, this time of twelve. He wipes his forehead with a white towel before doing it again.

Holding a walker tightly with both hands, he moves up and

down the hallway with legs showing less wobble but with arms that still struggle as he recovers and rests his arms by leaning against a wall. An orderly walks by, putting his hand up in the air. John gives him a tired but motivating high five as he wipes his dripping face with his sky-blue pajama sleeves and goes back down the hallway again.

John looks at a picture of Ginger and strokes the silver frame. He smiles and then places it on his night-stand along with the framed images of four other women that are carefully positioned on the wood-stained surface, the frozen, staggered memories are displayed in no order of time and in no preference to one another. He slips on a pair of classic white sneakers and stands up on his own, his legs straight and stiff and without the slightest wiggle.

The big black lady forks a piece of broccoli and puts it in her mouth, chewing it with strain as much as she can before washing the mouthful with a bottle of Mountain Dew. John stands behind her in the doorway, with nothing more than a thin cane aiding him.

The black woman looks around and smiles at him, clapping. The rest of the breakfast regulars turn around and clap as well, giving him much-deserved recognition. He smiles to them all and walks over.

The nurse looks on and watches him eat his food without effort. John looks back at her and smiles as he finishes his last bite.

He wipes his mouth and stands up.

"I'm proud of you, John."

"I'm proud of me too," he says with a smile.

She smiles back.

"I won't be here tomorrow…"

He looks at her and then walks over and kisses her on the cheek.

"You are the sweetest... sweetest nigger-child I've ever met... don't you go changing for nobody," he says with a kindness that carries with it not the slightest of foul intents.

She smiles and wipes a tear from her eyes.

"Take care.... and eat your broccoli," he says, making her chuckle.

He walks by the front hallway and sees a beautiful sil- ver-haired woman exiting a large SUV. She is swarmed by a gang of young sons who help her exit the vehicle while an even young- er looking group of grandsons unload the vehicle of its many pieces of luggage.

John looks on and smiles, slowly sipping his coffee with de- termination.

John lies on his back with his eyes closed and face frozen and still, his mouth open.

A nurse walks in.

"John..." the nurse says.

He doesn't respond. The nurse sighs a little with anxiety."

"John!" she says again.

He gives no response.

Finally she walks up to him and shakes him.

"John?"

His eyes open and she jumps back, startled that he actually woke up.

He flashes her an ornery grin.

"John... you no-good piece-a-shit," she says, hitting him with a pillow as he laughs.

"Hell... you were more scared when I woke up," he says, blocking her pillow beating.

John leans against the wall of the shower and lets the hot water cook his back red as the smoking liquid rolls across his face and drips off his lips as he stares at the water swirling around the drain.

He sits in a chair, his black dress socks up to his knees, squeezing a hand gripper, his plump old veins pronounced as they swell against his thin, blotchy skin. He puts on a pair of black dress slacks that look slick and wrinkle-free and a white button-down shirt. In the mirror he flips a blood-red tie across his face as he creates a perfect Windsor knot with no effort before draping on a matching black sports coat that fits him like a glove. He coats his thin grey hair with a dime-size dollop of pomade, slicking it back with a red comb. He slips on shoes that shine black like a freshly waxed Mercedes and grabs a blood-red rose that matches his tie.

The new silver-haired woman sits quietly in the commons area drinking coffee and listening to Martin and his friends flirt obnoxiously with a Yankee dialect that makes the woman grimace behind her friendly smile.

John walks into the room with the confidence of a general and the look of a mafia leader. The woman takes notice as he walks right up to her table, making the three other guys stop their conversation and look up in fearful respect.

"John." Martin says.

"Martin." John says as he stares at him hard.

John subtly nods with his head, and two of the guys meekly stand up and leave.

Martin holds out for a moment, but without his friends, John's aggressive stare seems too much as he deflates.

"It was nice meeting you Reva," Martin says, shaking her hand.

"The pleasure… it was all mine" the woman says with a deeply lingering Southern drawl, one that makes John grin.

Martin leaves.

John sits down and hands her a rose. She smiles and smells it.

"Reva?" he says.

"John?" she says, stretching the short name with her thick southern drawl as one of the staff sets a hot cup of 2 creams-one sugar coffee right in front of him.

Thanks Darlin'," he says as he pulls out a silver flask and pours a bit of liquor in the smoking liquid. He looks at her. She smiles and pushes her shallow cup over to him. He poisons hers as well.

"My momma always told me… *Reva baby… trouble's never gonna stop knocking' on your door…* I guess she was right."

"Troubles always put a smile on your face?" he asks.

She nods and takes her spiked bit of warm coffee down.

"Perhaps one more round," she says, sliding her empty mug next to him and gazing vulnerably.

He nods his head and smiles.

"Yeah… Perhaps."

The Last Summer Snow

When the cottonwoods bloom and the warm summer air whips their little fuzz balls around, it's like it's flurrying in July. The white snow dances through the air, immune to the brutality of the sun. It is one of the most beautiful things I've ever seen. I often stand outside in the middle of my little postage stamp of claimed earth and let the cooked summer air heat me up like a giant blow dryer, while the scorching, dog-day snowstorm overtakes me with outstretched arms and a smile wide enough to taste the summer snow. As the soft flakes tickle my face and nose and while my eyelids blink rapidly, fending off the floating white intruders, my happiness remains even though it's become spiked with sadness. This is my last season: the final pages of my life.

I could tell you that I'm dying, but old people like me don't die. We just fade away, our layers slowly blown off like tumbleweeds in a slow, steady breeze: each seed representing a sister, a friend, a husband, or even a child that the wind carries into nothingness, the earth swallowing each of their lives into a void, turning them into just memories in our heads: one that, only if you're lucky, will stay there for a while.

I wish I could tell you I'm grateful to be so mentally healthy, that I count my blessings every day, that I'm not lying in a nursing home bed with a soiled diaper and a drooling chin, but sometimes I envy that blankness. I have often found myself intrigued at the zombie-like stare my friend used to give me when I'd go visit her. I'd watch those miracle medications putting her diseased memory on a permanent pause, keeping her from her sobering stench of piss, shit and regurgitated Ensure. I figured that if the magical stuff circling her veins could numb her mind to where the diarrhea in her diaper felt like a soothing heat pad and the living hell in which she was rotting seemed like a weekend beer buzz in Maui, it might not be all that bad. Ignorance is bliss after all.

Instead I just sit at home, with a mind as sharp as a razor, but with a body as old as my ancient nemesis, gravity. Yet, all I do is play his game, rocking back and forth in my rickety old rocker, addicted to Earth's lethal force, allowing it to continue to brittle my bones and shrink my muscles. I spend my days there, watching the sun's reflection light up my entire life. Yellow beams illuminate the glass of the cheap picture frames that litter my walls and clutter my end tables, containing in them loved ones that are so beautifully frozen in time that over the years, they have become nothing more than teases. They are trapped in their two-dimensional world, preventing them from ever holding me again, or kissing me or touching me, or telling me how much they love me. Their happy moment in time is just a reminder of another layer of my soul removed. It doesn't mean I don't try though. Sometimes my loneliness overtakes me, and I grab a picture from off the wall and hold it as tightly against my chest as I can, crying and hoping for them to give me the comfort they used to, but I never feel anything but sharp wooden corners of the frame and the cool tear-covered glass of their flat prison.

I sometimes wonder if I'm being punished, or if I did something wrong. I shouldn't be living this long. I avoided vegetables my entire life, and the only exercise I ever got was walking around the house in a nicotine-filled panic trying to find my lighter. Everyone lied to me. They told me this stuff would kill me, that it would put me in an early grave, but they were wrong. One by one, they all left me. My parents have been gone so long, I've forgotten the sound of their voices. And my sisters - they were picked off one by one in a two-year time frame. My husbands - all of three of them - are also gone. A combined married life of over sixty years, and I never once got a divorce. I was always faithful, but despite this, all of them found a way to leave me with the ultimate exit strategy. And my friends, they're all long gone. Even my enemies, the people that I loved to hate, the ones that angered me to no end but gave my life that much-needed drama, they are also gone, every one.

Then, one day, my longevity stopped being annoying and just became a cruel gift. My child, the little baby boy that I had raised and loved, kept growing up, until one day he started growing old. He got older and older, and then his heart gave out. Parents shouldn't bury their children, but I did, and the worst part about it was that his death wasn't a surprise, and it wasn't a tragedy to anyone but me. People who die in their seventies are not tragedies, rather they are just a part of life: Mother Nature's *out with the old, in with the new* philosophy. The biggest part of me died that day, but I wish all of me would have.

I hated God for a long time after that. I stopped going to church and even read a satanic cult book once just to piss Him off. But that was a long time ago, and now, I think we're okay. We talk from time to time. Well, I talk and He listens, or at least I think He does, and it helps. Sometimes when the air in the house gets chilly and my old, aching muscles cringe at the thought of walking across the room to get a blanket, the sun breaks free from the clouds and comes through my spotty, dirty window and radiates me, warming me to the bone and wrapping me in a heated cocoon that feels like a thousand protective hugs, easing me into a deep slumber, I know it's Him. I know it's God putting his arms around me and letting me know that it's okay and that he still loves me.

I'm not entirely alone. I do have one grandson. I don't know him very well and he doesn't know me that much either, but it's not because we don't love each other, it's just that he is so very young and it's hard to talk to a thirty-year-old when you've reached triple digits.

I had a birthday a couple of weeks ago, and he came down to celebrate with me. It was just him and me in this old museum of a house, feeding the walls with more noise than it has heard in months. He told me that birthday candles only come in packs of twenty, and that the store only had three packs left, so he just decorated the cheap grocery store vanilla cake with all of them. As he lit the candles and turned the cake into a bakery bonfire, he sang me happy birthday out-of-tune, and I smiled and laughed at him. He looked so much like my son that it was like going back in time.

He pushed forward a poorly wrapped present. It was flat and obviously another old picture frame. But when he said, "Happy Birthday, Granny," with such a proud look, it piqued my interest. I opened it up and see a beautiful blond-haired, blue-eyed baby boy in the nice, high quality picture frame. "It's your great grandson," he said, grinning from ear to ear like a proud father. "Yeah, you're a great grandmother, now!" he said, confirming. I looked at the picture again, at that smiling baby face and began to cry with joy. "That's so great!" I say to him as we embrace, and he hugs me gently as if my bones were made of Styrofoam. "Do you want me to hang it up with the others?" he asked. "No, No! I'll just hold onto this one. This picture is different!" I said, wrapping my arms around it like it was a block of gold.

He looked out the window and noticed the cottonwoods blooming. He told me it was snowing and invited me outside. He helped me up and walked my ancient body out on the porch. We watched the cottonwood seeds litter the sky and tickle our skin, and I watched him smiling, enjoying it as much as I do.

"Your father and I used to come out here and do the same thing," I said to him.

"I know," he responded. He then asked me if next summer I would consider moving out of state and closer to him. He tells me he would put me in a nice home where I could meet lots of new friends and I would be close to him and my great grandson. I told him, "Maybe," and he didn't push the issue.

The truth is I'm too old to meet new friends, too old to start anything over, and I won't be here next summer anyway, this I know. One thing I've learned is that life, in a way, can be over even when you're still breathing. It's like you enter death's waiting room, where life slows to a crawl. I don't know why my entire life, until this point, has moved so fast and then suddenly hit the brakes. Maybe the Almighty sometimes puts life in slow motion towards the end so you can soak it up more. So that, on days like this, you can really take time to enjoy it.

I don't know what lies on the other side, but I know that I'll never be here again. Maybe every time a cottonwood seed tickles my nose and makes me smile, God is telling me to enjoy it. That when the hot summer wind whips the fuzz balls around me, I believe it's Him reminding me to embrace life and relish this beautiful waiting room He has created for me. And maybe, He's letting me know that, even in the winter of my life, I can still enjoy one last summer snow.

First and foremost, I would like to thank my Publisher, *Montag Press* for their tireless effort in helping make Wound and Suture something I am very proud of. I would also like to thank Bethney and Reva, two of the most outstanding, wounded, angry, disturbed, soul crushing, artistic and intelligent pair of critical eyes that no writer wants to have, but every writer needs to have. I would also like to thank the creators of Prolixin for slowing down the never ending story machine in my head and making the voices whisper instead of shout. To the makers of Diet Dr. Pepper, Rooster booster, Monster or any other cheap stimulant for helping keep the hair-pulling consistent throughout the night. For full contact fighting, the only pain that cures my pain. To the purveyors of fine internet porn everywhere. And last but not least to my inner demons, the hauntings that never quiet until I write them down. Without their pestering I would be so lonely.

-W.A Coleman

W.A. Coleman is a native of Tulsa, Oklahoma.
He is married and has a son.